Accidentally Evil

Don't miss the start of Hallie's adventure:

The XYZs of Being Wicked

Accidentally Evil

Lara Chapman

ALADDIN MIX
NEW YORK   LONDON   TORONTO   SYDNEY   NEW DELHI

ALADDIN M!X
Simon & Schuster Children's Publishing Division
1230 Avenue of the Americas, New York, NY 10020
This Aladdin M!X edition April 2015
Text copyright © 2015 by Lara Chapman
Cover illustrations copyright © 2015 by Coco Masuda
Also available in an Aladdin hardcover edition.
All rights reserved, including the right of reproduction in whole or in part in any form.
ALADDIN is a trademark of Simon & Schuster, Inc., and related logo is a registered trademark of Simon & Schuster, Inc.
ALADDIN M!X and related logo are registered trademarks of Simon & Schuster, Inc.
For information about special discounts for bulk purchases, please contact
Simon & Schuster Special Sales at 1-866-506-1949 or business@simonandschuster.com.
The Simon & Schuster Speakers Bureau can bring authors to your live event. For more information or to book an event contact the Simon & Schuster Speakers Bureau at 1-866-248-3049 or visit our website at www.simonspeakers.com.
Cover designed by Laura Lyn DiSiena
The text of this book was set in Fairfield.
Manufactured in the United States of America 0315 OFF
10 9 8 7 6 5 4 3 2 1
Library of Congress Control Number 2014960003
ISBN 978-1-4814-0111-1 (hc)
ISBN 978-1-4814-0110-4 (pbk)
ISBN 978-1-4814-0112-8 (eBook)

For Mom and Dad . . .
who taught me that giving up was never a choice

Acknowledgments

Thank you, thank you . . .

Holly Root, I can't imagine my career without you steering the ship. You were gifted with the ultimate trifecta—wit, wisdom, and wicked-good instincts—and I'm so honored to call you my agent.

Alyson Heller, Teresa Ronquillo, and the many others at Aladdin M!X who had a hand in bringing *Accidentally Evil* to life and then to the shelves . . . a million thanks wouldn't be enough. Every single person I've worked with has been as enthusiastic about Hallie and the girls as I am. Thank you for welcoming us into the Aladdin M!X family!

Coco Masuda, your work on the covers of *The XYZs of Being Wicked* and *Accidentally Evil* is nothing short of pure genius. Thank you for sharing your talent with my readers and me.

To my Suh-weet Success Sisters—Alex Ratcliff, Kimberly Belle, and Koreen Myers . . . Regardless of where we are, what we're writing, or what's going on in our lives, you will always be my favorites. I'm so thankful to have made that trip to the mountain. Here's to a lifetime of trips together. Mwah!

Bill, Caleb, Laney, and Weston . . . no amount of success would have meaning without you. You make me happier than I deserve and stronger than I thought possible. You are my everything.

Two of my students inspired the creation of Hallie, who's smart, funny, and genuinely good. Megan R. and Jackie G., you are amazing young women and I can't wait to see how you leave your mark on this crazy world.

To my readers . . . you are the reason I write, and I am so thankful you've spent some time with Hallie and the girls. Each one of you has been blessed with special gifts that can change the lives of others.

Embrace your power. Live out loud.

One

Unless you've been blessed with the gift of premonition, there's no preparing for your second first day at Dowling.

Last year I entered the Dowling Academy School of Witchcraft in fear, all sweaty hands and pounding heart.

Last year I hauled my impossibly heavy trunk to my room. Last year everything—and I mean *everything*—changed.

I walk under the large oak tree, now fully aware what happens beneath it. Blessings and socials, and darker things I've yet to see, I'm sure. My senses, dulled by the scorching Texas heat and never-ending summer days, now zap to life.

There's a bounce in my step as I keep myself from

running inside to find my best friend, Ivy. It's been two long months since I last saw her. FaceTime just isn't the same as being with someone. It was impossible to talk about boys or magic or gossip without one of our mothers eavesdropping. So we had to settle for late-night texting to talk about the good stuff.

I pat the iPhone in my back pocket, happy I'm allowed to have it. Last year I was a Seeker, which means I was a beginner. Seekers have almost no privileges. No phones, no television, no computers. It was a lot like prison, but with better food.

This is my second year, and I'm a Crafter, which means I know what my gift is (that's a really long story) and I've passed the Seeker exam. I'm a long way from being a real witch, though. That takes years.

I stop in front of the massive Dowling doors that once seemed so forbidding. Just me. No parents. No trunk. *No nerves.*

What a difference a year makes.

I pull the door open and let the cool air wash over me. Before I'm fully inside the building, I hear Miss A call my name.

"Hallie!"

My eyes adjust to the dim lighting, and my dorm mom's face becomes clear. A huge smile stretches across my face. Last year I accidentally made her dye her hair orange and she hasn't changed it since. Beneath that tangled curly mess of shocking hair is the face I've missed so much. She was only my dorm mom a year, but we have a special connection.

She pulls me into a big, squishy hug. "Looky here, looky here! Aren't you a sight for sore eyes!"

I laugh and pull out of the embrace. "I missed you too, Miss A."

I've tried to forget that Miss A won't be my dorm mom this year. All the other dorm moms are überserious and a little bit scary. Miss A's like the crazy grandmother at family reunions. Her face is painted too brightly, and her lipstick is always smeared across her teeth. But you just know she's always going to be there for you.

"Is Ivy here yet?" I ask.

She checks her watch before answering. "Her mama called and said they were running late. Should be here in about an hour."

I try not to look too disappointed. I'm excited about seeing Miss A, but Ivy is the one I really want to see.

When you go through what we did last year, you're more than just friends. You're sisters.

I glance at the staircase and smile. "Our trunks are here."

"You betcha," Miss A says, smiling.

The trunks whiz up the stairs, two feet off the ground, unassisted. When we witnessed it last year, Ivy passed out. She would've hit the floor and split her head open if Miss A hadn't frozen her midfall. Magic saved the day— something that would happen many times after.

"Didn't I tell you this would happen for you as a Crafter?" Miss A asks.

"You did." I am mesmerized by the trunks and wonder if mine has already been delivered to my room.

"It's already in there," Miss A answers.

It takes me a second to remember that my thoughts project. I'd gotten used to no one hearing my thoughts all summer. I kind of liked it that way.

"If you don't want me reading your thoughts, you better get busy figuring out how to close that brain of yours off from me," she says with a wink. "And everyone else."

"Yes, ma'am," I answer. There are a lot of things I still don't understand about my gift. Or gifts. With the gift of inheritance, I can acquire gifts from other witches. Last year I accidentally picked up the gift of mind manipulation. That means sometimes people hear my thoughts about what I think they should do, and then they do it. But they don't realize I'm the one who gave them the idea. That's how Miss A got the orange hair. It's kind of like subliminal messages, only I have almost no control over who hears what. I'm hoping to work that out this year.

"Better get your room assignment and settle in. Invocation is at five thirty in the Gathering Circle."

The Gathering Circle—or GC—is the main meeting room at Dowling. It's the only room in the building big enough to hold all of the Dowling girls. This is my second year, but there are some girls who have been here five years. Even longer if they're full-fledged witches.

Some Dowling students never leave—they return year after year to teach future witches.

I walk to the welcome desk, manned by two fourth circle witches. That's what I'll be next year if I make it through this one.

"Hi, Hallie," one of the girls says. I don't know her, so I'm surprised she knows who I am. She hands me my ID, which holds a picture taken of me today. I have no clue how they do it, but they manage to get a picture of us the day we arrive, without us knowing. And voila! It appears on our badge. That kind of thing is hard to get used to.

Just as I'm about to walk away, the other girl sneers at me. "Good luck this year, Hallie. Not that you're going to need it." The last part is said under her breath, but I hear it anyway.

Of course they know who I am.

Everyone knows who I am.

I am the first student at Dowling to have the gift of inheritance since High Priestess Dannabelle Grimm was here in the 1800s. Apparently that's kind of a big deal. All I really wanted to be was a hedge witch like my great-great-grandmother, mixing herbs and potions to heal and to cast spells. But I got a lot more than I bargained for.

I walk away and smile back at the girls, whose faces wear frozen, fake smiles. Miss A said people would be jealous. She was right.

I look at my badge. My room number is 202.

I climb the stairs two at a time, anxious to see the room I'll share with Ivy. During the first year, Seekers are required to room with whomever Dowling assigns us to.

For me that meant my worst enemy of all time, Kendall Scott. Being able to choose my roommate this year was a big deal. Huge.

I hit the top of the stairs and find the hallway crammed with girls talking, hugging, and snapping fingers. Small bursts of magic appear as girls show off their still-new skills. One girl keeps walking through a wall and back again. Back and forth, back and forth, her friends begging to see her do it "just one more time." It's hard not to watch her, because it's crazy cool. A different girl farther down the hallway has accidentally (I think) frozen a girl's legs in a block of ice. There are probably six or seven girls around the frozen girl, chipping at the ice.

I can't stop smiling. Even though it's a madhouse, it's my madhouse. Home.

"Hallie!" Dru Goode, still a foot shorter than everyone else, pushes her way through the cluster of girls to get to me.

She breaks through, and I smile when I see her. Her perfect white teeth are in direct contrast to her dark skin and black curly hair. It's impossible not to love her. I hug her close, then look behind her.

"Where's Jo?"

Dru shrugs. "I haven't seen her. What room are you in?"

"Room 202," I tell her.

She pushes my shoulder so hard, I nearly fall. "Get out! We're in 204! We're neighbors!"

"You're stronger than you look," I tell her, laughing.

I send a silent thank-you to Miss A. I know she's the reason our rooms are next to each other.

I look at the room numbers on the wall and realize I'm standing in front of my door. "Have you gone into your room yet?" I ask Dru.

"Yep," she says. "Same as last year."

I swipe my ID in the door scanner, and the door unlocks. I push it open and—just as Dru said—the rooms are identical to last year's. The only difference is a big one. There's a laptop on each of our desks.

I spin to face Dru. "I didn't know we were getting laptops!"

"Me either," she says. "But don't get too excited. I hear we have superlimited Internet access."

"Still, we can at least check our e-mail." I look at Dru. "Can't we?"

Dru nods. "Miss A said we could. But no Facebook."

Good. As long as we have e-mail, I'm golden.

My trunk sits in front of one of the beds. Ivy's trunk is already here too. "Your trunk make it here okay?"

Dru nods. "I don't even care how it happens. I'm just glad I didn't have to haul it upstairs. Those trunks are heavy!"

There are definitely perks to being a witch.

"I wish I'd brought my glow-in-the-dark pj's from home. They've got a picture of my family on them," I say.

"Your pj's?" Dru asks, sneaky smile on her face. "At home? Two hundred long miles from here?"

"Dru, are you sure you know what you're doing?"

She puts her fists on her hips. "I'll pretend you didn't just say that."

I put my hands up in apology. "You're right. What was I thinking?" Last year Dru's gift of conjuration came in handy when she produced a curling iron before the dance at Riley Academy, where I met Cody.

Cody Ray. The "it" guy at Dowling's brother school. We met at last year's social, and no matter how hard I tried to discourage him, he was glued to me all night long. I've seen girls ignore their friends because of boys, and I swore I'd never be one of those girls. Besides, life at Dowling is complicated enough. The last thing I need is a distraction. But that's exactly what I have.

Dru closes her eyes, puts her fingers in snapping position. She peeks out at me. "Where do you keep your pj's at home?"

"My dresser. Bottom drawer."

She closes her eyes again, takes a deep breath. She whispers words I can't hear, and tiny colorful sparks dance off her fingertips.

I look at my desk, then high-five Dru.

Sitting there beside my laptop are the pj's I left behind.

Two

My clothes are unpacked, my uniforms hung. Decorative pillows are on the bed and family pictures are on the dresser. The only thing missing is Ivy. I look at the watch on my wrist. She should already be here. I decide to check in with Miss A to see if she's heard from her. My nose is just inches from the door when it swings open and smacks me right in the face.

"Yoooooooowww!" I yell. I put my hand over my now bleeding nose.

"Hallie! Oh my gosh, I'm so sorry!" Ivy comes through the door and guides me to the bathroom. She's half-laughing as she grabs one of the hand towels from the cabinet. "What were you doing there?"

I sit on the toilet and tilt my head back. "I was trying to leave."

"Pinch your nose," she says.

I do as she says as she stands over me, holding the towel over my face. "Been working out?" I ask.

She laughs, and the sound of her voice makes me forget the throbbing in my nose. I didn't realize how much I missed her.

"No," she says. "You know me better than that."

"Well, you sure swung that door open like a heavyweight champ."

She removes the towel. "When did you become so fragile?"

"Very funny." I sit up and look at myself in the mirror. But I can't focus on my nose with Ivy looking like that. "Your hair!"

She tosses the towel into the hamper and rubs soap onto her hands. "Like it?"

Last year Ivy's hair stayed in long braids. I once tricked her into leaving it down and was stunned by how full and curly it was. It's still the perfect shade of auburn, but the braids are gone. Soft curls frame her face and rest on her shoulders.

"Wow," I say.

"Is that a good 'wow' or a what-were-you-thinking 'wow'?"

"Are you kidding me? Your hair is freaking awesome!"

She gives me an easy smile. "You're leaking again."

I grab a tissue and hold it to my nose. When I compare my own reflection to Ivy's, I feel like I am behind. My straight brown hair has grown over the summer. But I still wear it pulled back in a headband. Simple. Easy. And suddenly childish.

"You okay?" she asks. "I'm sorry I hit you with the door. I didn't know you were standing on the other side."

I follow Ivy out of the bathroom and into our bedroom. "I was leaving to look for you."

"Lie down," she says, pointing at my bed. "Keep pinching."

I do as she says and watch her drag a duffel bag into the room.

"What took you so long?" I ask.

Ivy gives me a shrug. "Just running late." There's a distance to her voice, but she doesn't give me time to ask what's wrong. "How long have you been here?"

"A couple of hours. You missed the flying trunks."

"I saw all of that that I needed to see last year, even if I don't remember everything that happened." She drops to the bed and lies back. "Jeez, it's good to be back."

"I didn't think summer was ever going to end." I pull the tissue from my nose. "There. It's stopped bleeding."

"Good. Help me unpack."

I'm kind of OCD—okay, a lot OCD—so I'm happy to take over. I make quick work of hanging her uniforms and organizing her dresser.

She pulls school supplies from her bag and freezes midturn when she gets a good look at her desk. "Whoa! Laptops?"

"I know. I didn't realize we were getting them either."

"Very nice," she says, then more quietly, "Have you seen them?"

Them. She doesn't have to say the names of our enemies for me to know who she's asking about. Kendall and her partner in crime, the equally awful Zena Fallon.

I shake my head. "Just Dru. She and Jo are next door."

"Yes!" She tosses the things in her hands onto the bed. "Let's go see them. I can finish later."

It pains me to leave with her stuff all over the room, but I follow her anyway. The hallway is empty—at this point most of the girls are getting unpacked before invocation. The first night at Dowling is a long one. Ivy knocks two times on Dru and Jo's door, and it opens almost immediately. What follows is a mix of screams, laughs, and hugs. As Seekers the four of us stuck together, and it made the year bearable. Fun, even, on some days. We had a common interest last year—bringing down Kendall and Zena. I suspect we'll have the same mission this year.

Kendall Scott has hated me since a third-grade sleepover turned bad. From that day on she made it her personal mission to make sure my life was miserable. As luck would have it, she is also a Dowling descendent, and we were forced to room together last year.

Zena Fallon was Ivy's roommate. She is also the daughter of Dowling's headmistress. Kendall and Zena quickly connected and brought out the evil in one another.

"Man, you two have been busy!" I say. Dru and Jo's room is decorated in bold colors—hot pink, lime green, and neon orange the same shade as Miss A's hair. I picture our mess of a room and shiver.

Ivy reads my mind. "Relax. We'll get our room done tonight."

"Hallie! What happened to your nose?" Dru asks, just

now realizing it's twice its normal size and still growing.

My hand goes to my nose, and I wince in pain. "Welcome-back gift from my roomie."

Ivy eyes are apologetic. "I said I was sorry."

I finally get a good look at Jo. Over the summer she went from pimples and do-nothing hair to model-worthy glam. Blemish free, just-right makeup, and hair that looks like Rumpelstiltskin himself spun it from gold.

"Holy Saffra, Jo!" I say. "You look great!"

Her face flushes. "One of my cousins spent the summer with us to attend cosmetology school, and I became her project. And this is what happened."

"Well, I guess she got herself an A!"

"She even took me to her school to show me off, like I was a new puppy or something." She rolls her eyes like she was embarrassed, but I know how much that must have meant to her.

Dru leans in close, her voice a whisper. "Have you seen them?"

We all look at each other, shaking our heads.

"I don't blame Kendall for staying out of sight," Ivy says, her voice deep with smugness. "Wonder if she's learned how to talk with her new tongue."

We burst into uncontrollable laughter.

Last year, when I was still testing out my gift of transformation, I cast a spell for Kendall's true heart to be shown. I had thought the old Kendall—the sweet, funny Kendall I had known before third grade—was in there somewhere. When her true heart was shown, her tongue forked like a snake's. The last time I saw her, she was impossible to understand because her tongue kept slipping out and searching the air. It flicked just like a snake's. As a rule I'm terrified of snakes. But I can handle Kendall. I think.

"So, Hallie," Jo says with a knowing smile. "Talked to Cody?"

My face flushes red-hot. "No."

"You're the worst liar I've ever known. It's written all over your face."

Ivy examines my face. "You're right, Jo. She gets that weird little tic in the corner of her eye." She puts her finger on me, and I pull back. "See?" she asks. "Right there."

"And her face gets all red and splotchy," Jo adds.

I instinctively bring my hands to my face. "Excuse me, but I'm standing right here."

Dru crosses her arms. "Then come clean. Did you talk to him?"

"We e-mailed," I say.

"Well?" Ivy said. "About what?"

Family. School. Witchcraft. Everything.

I shrug. "Stuff."

Dru gives me an *I'm not buying it* look. "How often did you hear from him?"

"I don't know. It's not like I kept count." *219 times.*

"And?" Ivy pushes.

I force conviction into my voice. No one needs to know I really like him. I've barely admitted it to myself. "And nothing. We're just friends."

"We're supposed to have more events with Riley as Crafters," Ivy says. "My sister let that slip."

Ivy's sister graduated from Dowling but chose to live a regular "civilian" life. Now that I have them, I can't imagine leaving my gifts behind, letting them go dormant. But that's just me. I can see how being a witch might not be for everyone.

There's a knock at the door, and all four of us turn, waiting for the door to open. Miss A can enter without a key, and we aren't expecting anyone. But Miss A doesn't breeze through an opened door, and there's another knock. Then another. Each one harder than the last.

Dru walks to the door. She opens it forcefully, like she's trying to scare someone, just like Ivy opened the door earlier.

Standing on the other side of the door are the two people we like least.

Kendall and Zena.

If possible, they're even prettier than they were last year.

Kendall speaks first, all Suzy Sunshine like we're BFFs. "Hi, girls!"

Looks like she mastered the whole forked-tongue thing just fine. I try to glimpse it in her mouth, but she's too fast.

"Looks like everyone made it back okay," Zena says, eyes narrowing critically. I know she notices Jo's transformation, but she'd rather jump into a boiling cauldron than compliment her.

Kendall's eyes land on mine. Her lips lift slowly, and I brace myself. I know that look. She's a jungle cat ready to pounce on her prey.

"Oh my God, Hallie," she says. Her voice is part

sneer, part "gotcha." "What is wrong with your *nose?*"

"Shut up, Kendall," Ivy says.

"Touchy," Kendall says, entirely too happy for my liking.

"At least it's temporary," I shoot back. "How's that new tongue working out for you?"

Zena jumps in before Kendall can answer. "Hope you girls can keep up this year. It will be our hardest, after all."

I put my hands on my hips. "Maybe for some. Not for me. Not for us."

They cross their arms simultaneously, like they've rehearsed it a million times in the mirror.

"Your lips are moving, but all I hear is 'blah, blah, blah,'" Zena says.

Dru puts her hand on the door. "Ta-ta," she says, as sweet as pie.

Then slams the door in their faces.

Three

The four of us walk into the Gathering Circle for invocation, less anxious than last year, but my nerves are still jumpy. It feels like my heart is in my throat. The GC is one of my favorite places at Dowling. There's a reverence to it I find comforting. Knowing that thousands of Dowling descendants have congregated in this room makes me feel connected in a way that just feels right.

The headmistress is at the door, greeting every girl by name. Even the new ones. She's exactly as I remember—black silk hair, thin body in perfect proportions, and eyes that see deep inside a person's soul.

She lays a hand on my shoulder in greeting. The alien greeting, I called it last year.

"Welcome back, Hallie," she says. Her eyes linger on me so long, it gets awkward. I force myself to stand tall. No squirming.

"Thank you, Headmistress."

I follow Ivy inside to the second row from the top. Last year, as Seekers, we sat in the top row. Each year, as we progress, we descend to the next row, then the next, until we are in the first row circling the triangular stage in the center of the room. I'm a long way from the first row, but I'm grateful I'm not at the top anymore.

I check out this year's Seekers as we walk to our seats. I give them encouraging smiles because I know how nervous they are. Nervous enough to puke. Their tight-lipped scared-speechless faces say it all.

The room hums in whispers and muffled laughs. It fills quickly and the candles dim. The dorm mothers sit on the stage, and I feel a twinge of sadness. I never would have survived last year without Miss A. She literally saved my life. How can I get through this year with anyone else? The other dorm mothers are all sharp angles and dark features. Then there's Miss A. A green crystal butterfly clip pulls curly bangs away from her face. The gems sparkle and clash with her hair. But it's classic

Miss A. I'm surprised Dowling tolerates her eccentricity. They are all about conformity. Something tells me there's a story behind my favorite dorm mom. Maybe this is the year I'll find out what that story is.

Zena and Kendall enter the room at the last possible moment, and the doors close behind them with a thump. They sit on the end of the row and keep their eyes straight ahead. They say nothing. It's textbook Intimidation 101. But I know the truth about Kendall, and I know the truth about me. And all the glares and cold shoulders in the world can't change the fact that I'm more powerful than she will ever be.

My mind wanders as the headmistress takes the stage and introduces herself. If I didn't know any better, I'd say it was the exact same speech she gave last year. Complete with sweeping arm motions and a booming, theatrical voice. Her makeup is dramatic, and she oozes authority. No one does scary witch better than Headmistress Fallon.

As she raises her arms, her wooden wand in one hand, the candle flame in front of her stretches, stretches, stretches until it's nearly as tall as she is.

"So cool," Ivy says under her breath.

And it is. Way cool.

The headmistress's voice is solemn but loud.

"Dowling sisters, your powers proclaim,
your right of lineage by Saffra's name.
A witch can give success in love,
curse or bless through Saffra above.
Speak to beasts and spirits alike,
command the weather, cast out a blight.
Read the heavens and stars of the night,
divine the future and give good advice.
Conjure treasure and bring fortune to bear,
heal the sick and kill despair.
This is your birthright to have and to share.
Blessings, my sisters;
may the spirits be fair."

She lowers her hands, and the flame of the candle lowers with them. The smug look on her face says she hasn't grown tired of that little trick. A crowd-pleaser, my dad would call it.

The thought of my dad drives a blade of sadness through me. I love Dowling, but I miss my family when I'm gone.

The headmistress rambles on and on and on about how wonderful Dowling is and how this is going to be the best year in Dowling history.

She stops abruptly, then clears her throat. "Well . . . I guess I'm rambling a bit. I do get excited at the beginning of the year."

My eyes shoot up, and I remember too late that the headmistress is clairaudient, which makes her one of the people who can hear my thoughts. I have to learn how to keep my thoughts hidden. I've tried—over and over— without success. It's only a million times harder than it sounds.

"Before we dismiss, I'd like to introduce our dorm mothers."

The headmistress turns to the women behind her, and I swear I see her shake her head at the sight of Miss A. Lucky Seekers. It would almost be worth repeating my first year to have her again. Other than Miss A, I can hardly distinguish one dorm mother from the other, but I listen and watch anyway, waiting to see who we will get this year.

The headmistress is down to the last two dorm moms: Miss A and a toothpick of a woman next to her that I recognize from last year. "We've had a slight change in dorm mom assignments this year."

That gets our attention. Dowling doesn't do change.

"At her insistence, Miss A will be moving upstairs to stay with this year's Crafters."

I grab Ivy's hand and slap my other hand over my mouth to keep from screaming.

Miss A looks directly at me and winks.

Thank you. I think the words as clearly and deliberately as possible. I hope Miss A heard me, but I can't tell from looking at her face.

"You're welcome." The words are soft, but they aren't Miss A's. That's when I realize the headmistress said it. I have to stop projecting my thoughts. Emergencies only.

"Dorm mothers," the headmistress says, more loudly this time, intended for everyone to hear, not just me. "Please escort your girls to the dining room."

Zena and Kendall are the first to leave the room. They don't have the same affection for Miss A that Ivy and I do. Zena is old-school. She likes her witches threatening. Heartless.

Miss A has definitely got more of a Glenda-the-Good-Witch thing going.

We wait outside the CG for Miss A. When she comes through the doors, her smile is huge, her arms open wide. "How's that for a nice little surprise?"

She hugs Ivy and me.

"I have been so worried about this year's dorm mom."

"I'm aware. Your worry was projected to me all summer long. I finally had to do something about it."

My feet stop, but she keeps walking. How in the world did she hear me all the way from home? She looks at me over her shoulder. "Come on, Hallie. We have plenty of time to talk about it later. Let's eat. Smells like fried chicken."

I take a few quick steps to catch up, and go inside the dining room. The Crafter table is the second table in the room. Last year we had assigned seating. We sat with our roommates, which means I sat right next to Kendall. It was a long year. This year I'm grateful I get to sit next to my friends and as far away from Kendall and Zena as possible. My eyes scan the table, and I see Kendall and Zena sitting close to the head table, where the headmistress and dorm mothers eat. Suck-ups.

"Let's sit down here," Ivy says. "Next to Dru and Jo."

Ivy and I sit across from our friends. We pull our

chairs closer and water appears in our glasses as if it's being poured from an invisible pitcher.

Ivy points at her glass. "Okay. That's new."

"And coolio," Dru says, making us all laugh. Dru is the kind of girl who thinks everything is exciting. She may be small, but she speaks her mind and doesn't let anyone push her around. And sometimes she says the goofiest things. Like "coolio."

Napkins slide from the table into our laps. I hear the Seekers behind us gasp. I remember how shocking magic was to us last year. To be honest, it still amazes me. I don't really understand how magic works; it just does. And when it does, it's . . . coolio.

Fried chicken is swiftly delivered to everyone except me. My plate always comes last, which doesn't make any sense to me. I know a salad is easier to make than fried chicken. Today I get a large salad with exactly what I love on top. Carrots, bean sprouts, mushrooms, and olives. My favorite.

Jo looks at my food. "Maybe I should turn vegetarian. You know how long I'm going to have to run to work this off?"

"Tell them you converted over the summer. You won't

regret it." I stab my salad with a fork and sit back in my oversize, uncomfortable dining room chair. I chew slowly, taking in the view from my new seat. I can see Miss A if I lean back and twist my body to the left a little. Kendall and Zena are visible, but just barely.

I like this new arrangement quite a bit. I can stick close to the people I trust and block out the people I don't.

Perfection.

Four

Jo and Dru come to our room after dinner, and we busy ourselves getting the rest of Ivy's things unpacked and our room set up.

"Well, I wanted to let you know how the Summer Solstice Dance went. Since I was the only one out of us who could go . . . ," Dru begins. Her features are twisted into an uncharacteristic scowl.

"I couldn't help it," I tell her. "My family always goes to the beach the first week of summer."

The Summer Solstice dance. The last time I saw Cody, he said he'd see me there. I didn't even know what he was talking about until I got home for summer break and looked it up. I found out it's the first day of summer, and it's a celebration of the previous year's success, and a kickoff to the new year. Now prickles of excitement awake my arms, and my heart pumps a little faster at the thought of seeing Cody and not knowing what this year will bring.

"So, how was it?" I ask her, not that I really want to know.

Cody told me he was going, and Kendall wouldn't have missed it. Knowing those two were at the dance together makes me a little uneasy, but it's not like Cody and I are boyfriend and girlfriend. We're just . . . friends. Dru plops onto my bed. "Wellll . . ." She draws out the word, and her face returns to its normal, playful position. "Cody was there, for starters."

With those five words, both Ivy and Jo stop unpacking. They sit on Ivy's couch and get comfortable. I don't join them. The last thing I need is for them to notice how red my face gets when I talk about Cody. I keep my hands busy and continue to sort through Ivy's tangled jewelry. With my back to them, I hang or fasten each piece to her jewelry holder with surgical precision.

Ivy clears her throat. "Hallie."

I look over my shoulder. "What? I'm in the middle of something."

She huffs a big breath.

"Well," Dru says, ignoring my intentional absence from the conversation. "He has gotten taller. Like, three inches at least. And he just looks older. Wiser, maybe."

I grin to myself, my back still to my friends. Cody told me he'd been working out with his dad all summer. It makes me feel special to have known that before they did.

"Who else was there?" Jo asks.

"The evil stepsisters, of course."

Kendall and Zena.

Don't ask. Don't ask if Kendall and Cody danced.

I tell myself I don't want to know. Don't need to know. That it doesn't matter. Until last year I lived in Kendall's ominous shadow. I don't want to go back there again.

"So?" Ivy asks. I know it's coming, and I can't stop it. "Did Cody dance with them?"

Three sets of eyes burn a hole into the back of my neck, but I don't turn around.

"Yeah," Dru says, her voice low and soft. "He and Kendall danced a couple of times. It was hard to watch."

My stomach free-falls and lands somewhere near my toes. Of course he danced with her.

"Oh," Ivy says.

No one says anything for a few seconds. Seconds that feel like hours. Awkward silences always feel like time warps.

Dru clears her throat, nervous. "Kendall didn't have control of her tongue yet, though. It was hilarious to watch her attempt eating and drinking."

I smile big, and the flush on my face fades. This is the kind of gossip I want to hear, so I sit next to Dru on the bed. "Don't leave out a single detail."

"Well," she says. "She spilled water on herself all night long. If I didn't loathe her so much, I would have felt sorry for her. She couldn't keep that tongue in her mouth. It was huh-larious!"

We all laugh at the image of Kendall being less than perfect. Kendall will literally kill to maintain her perfect image.

"She seems better with it now," Jo says.

"Unfortunately," Ivy agrees.

"Here's the thing," Dru says. "She can only control it for a little while, according to the rumors I heard in the hallway. It's like her tongue does all the smelling for her or something like that. So it just kind of flicks out without warning."

I picture Kendall standing tall, full of herself, and her

newly forked tongue falling straight out of her mouth. Priceless.

I did everything I could to reconnect with Kendall last year, but she made it painfully clear that wasn't going to happen. Just remembering how she poisoned me last year makes my ears ring with anger.

"I hope that happens when I'm around to see it." It almost makes me wish we were still roomies so I could witness her struggle.

Almost.

"So what else happened at the dance?" I ask.

Dru shrugs. "Nothing, really. It was pretty tame. There weren't a ton of people there, and the music was kind of lame because the headmistress was in charge of it." She gives a dramatic eye roll that makes me laugh. "Lots of eighties music."

I don't tell them I actually like eighties music. Instead I laugh along with them. I wonder what secrets they keep from me? It's the first time I've really thought about it. My dad says everyone has secrets, and that secrets aren't always bad. Sometimes things are too special to share. That's how I feel about Cody right now.

Ivy's face darkens briefly. It returns to normal so

quickly, I wonder if it actually happened. That's the second time she's taken a mental break from a conversation today. She looks at me and smiles. It's the same genuine, in-control smile I remember from last year. Still, I can't shake that something's wrong.

"Ssh," Jo whispers. "They're in the hallway."

We look at the door, straining to hear what Jo can hear so clearly. She has the gift of clairaudience, which means she can hear things far away. She once heard me and Ivy talking about our favorite movies, and we were in a completely separate room.

"They stopped," she mouths, finger over her mouth to keep us quiet.

The room is so silent, I wonder if everyone else is holding their breath like me.

Jo leans back. "Okay," she says, her voice normal.

"What happened?" Ivy asks.

She shakes her head like she's freeing a cacophony of sounds from her ears. "I could hear them as clear as day."

"Hear *who*?" Dru asks. She is possibly the most impatient person I know.

"Kendall and Zena. They were talking in the hallway."

Ivy and I share a quick *This isn't good* look. With the

two of them rooming together this year, we will have to watch out for each other every single second of the day.

"And?" Dru's voice is insistent, and I'm afraid that if Jo doesn't answer in the next two seconds, Dru will fly out of the room and confront Kendall and Zena herself.

Jo giggles, a sound I haven't really heard before. She laughs infrequently at best, and even then, it's often forced. That girl is way too serious.

"First they were talking about what they're wearing tomorrow—"

"Um," I say, interrupting. "Our uniforms? Not much to decide."

"They were talking more about shoes and jewelry. And their hair."

Kendall has the kind of hair that is always perfect—it looks almost exactly like strands of gold and smells like coconut. She could roll out of bed and never put a brush through her hair and still look better than Barbie.

"That's all?" I ask.

Part of me is kind of disappointed they didn't say more. I was hoping to use Jo's gift to stay one step ahead of them.

"Pretty much," Jo says. She thinks for a second, then

snaps her fingers. "Oh yeah! They said that they'd 'show her' tomorrow."

My eyes practically fall out of my head. "That's the 'oh yeah'?"

Jo smiles, smug, satisfied. She loves to make me squirm.

"Is it me? Were they talking about me?" I ask.

She shrugs. "I don't know. They didn't say any names. But come on, Hallie. Who else would it be?"

She's right. I'm the only one they hate enough to target. I'd hoped that when my gift of inheritance was exposed and the true strength of my gift was understood, Kendall would leave me alone. Finally. But she only dug in more deeply, more convinced than ever that her purpose in life was to destroy me.

"I should have known she wouldn't change."

Ivy shifts to my bed and puts her arm around me. Her eyes are shiny, like she might cry. Her gift of empathy makes her hypersensitive to what other people are feeling, and it's even worse with me because we're so close.

"Don't worry," she says, pulling me in more tightly. "We're all in this together. She'll have to go through us to get to you."

"That's right," Dru says, resting a featherlight arm on my shoulder.

Jo doesn't say anything, but she doesn't have to. She is one of the most loyal people I've ever known. She'll be there.

I take a deep breath, will my nerves to calm down.

"It's one girl," I say to my friends. "How much harm can she really do?"

Five

Sitting in Lady Jennica Silver's class this morning, it's like I never even left. Lady Jennica is everyone's favorite teacher. She has turned the history of Dowling into something exciting and meaningful.

Lady Jennica isn't a traditional teacher. She doesn't look at us over her reading glasses, and she wouldn't be caught dead in a holiday sweater. Today she's wearing a silvery wispy dress. It has layers of thin material that is shorter in front but goes all the way to the floor behind her. I'm used to seeing her in black, but silver fits her better. And not because that's her last name. It just fits. Her black hair has grown and now reaches the middle of her back. It's held with a silver clip, and little pieces of hair that have come loose hang over her face. Last year she had purple highlights. This year they're red. But just a little. So little you can't really see it at first. But if you look closely enough, you can see it peeking through.

I was surprised someone as young as Lady Jennica was a teacher. But I found out later that Dowling hires Dowling graduates to teach. Only the best of the best are selected.

In the five minutes I've been sitting next to Ivy, the lights have gone off twice and the window shades have opened and closed at least a dozen times. A fireball hangs in the corner near the ceiling, and a girl stands below it looking guilty.

Class is just seconds away from starting. Kendall's and Zena's seats are, of course, empty. They are allergic to punctuality.

Lady Jennica snaps her fingers, and the door closes just as Zena and Kendall enter. The class snickers as the two girls attempt to look apologetic. But they're too arrogant to pull it off.

Kendall is still playing with her hair, twirling it around her fingers, when Lady Jennica tells them, "Consider this your one free pass for the year, girls."

Ha. There's no better way to start the day than seeing Kendall get in trouble.

Lady Jennica turns her attention to the rest of the class. "Welcome back, *Crafters*." She places special emphasis on our new level, and the room is full of smiles. "I am so glad you're back."

She fixes the blinds and dispels the fireball. "We'll get this under control this year."

Lady Jennica writes the word "Goals" on the board and swipes a sloppy line under it. "Let's talk about what you can expect this year."

I position my pencil over the first page in my brand-new spiral. I copy her word onto my paper and wait for more. I'm what some might call a bit of a teacher's pet. I prefer to think of myself as conscientious.

"You may have heard this will be your hardest year at Dowling."

The room gives her a collective nod.

"Relax," she says. "Every year feels like the hardest year. It's supposed to get tougher the longer you're here. That's how you know you're learning."

For some reason that doesn't make me feel better.

"So, let's talk about our major goal for this year."

She turns back to the board and writes in her familiar just-barely-legible handwriting.

"This year we'll learn more about our familial connections to Dowling." She faces us again. "This will involve more than producing a family tree. This will be in-depth genealogy research. The results . . ." She stops, looking for the right word. "The results are sometimes surprising. You know, when I was in this class at your age, I found out I was related to one of the dorm mothers. Funny, huh? So you never know what the research will drag up."

I personally detest surprises. I have to know what's going to happen, and when, and where, and how. Flying by the seat of my pants gives me hives.

Last year our major project was to research a High Priestess from Dowling's history. I was stuck doing the project with Kendall, but I got to choose the High Priestess. Dannabelle Grimm. Researching Dannabelle was not only interesting, but it was great for me when I found out she and I shared the same rare gift.

The rest of the class period is crammed with boring first-day-of-school stuff. Filling out papers, answering a questionnaire about our summer, that kind of thing. Just before class is over, Lady Jennica looks over to me and mouths, "Stay after." It's like a thousand moths have been set free in my stomach. Why does she want to see *me*?

When the bell rings, I tell Ivy I'll meet her in the next class.

"You sure? I can wait," she says.

"No, that's okay. I'll be right behind you." I hope.

I hang back as the room clears out, then walk to Lady Jennica's desk.

"Yes, ma'am?" I say. Manners matter, my dad says, and he's almost always right. It can be maddening how right he is.

She leans forward in her chair, hands clasped on the desk in front of her. "I am dying to know how your summer went."

I look at her, confused. "My summer?"

Her eyes widen. "Yeah. You know. It's those months that just went by when you lived with your parents."

Heat rushes to my face. "I know what summer is, but I'm not sure why you want to know about mine. Not that I mind telling you, of course."

Lady Jennica laughs lightly, like a wind chime tinkling in the breeze. "Hallie," she says, "I'm curious about your summer because of the gifts you inherited last year. I thought it might have made your summer . . . interesting, to say the very least."

"Oh," I say. "You mean the going invisible thing?"

She nods. "And the mind manipulation thing."

"And the transformation thing," I finish.

"Precisely," she says. "How'd it go?"

I shake my head. "I don't understand what you mean. I'm not trying to be dense, but I'm confused."

"Hallie," she says, her eyes tilting to a worried angle. "Did you try to use any of your gifts this summer? Or did they accidentally happen? Like when you accidentally made Miss A dye her hair?"

I think about the past couple of months, about our trip to the beach, and hanging out with my dog. I shake my head. "No, not really. Except this one time my mom said she was hungry for shrimp, but I was craving stir-fry. All of a sudden she changed her mind while we were driving and we ended up at Hong Kong Grill."

"That's all?" Lady Jennica asks. "Usually the girls have a rough time that first summer home. Their gifts always seem to leak out."

I laugh. "No, nothing like that happened. The rules say we aren't allowed to do that."

"Yeah, well . . . that doesn't mean it doesn't happen. We need to spend some time working on your control.

Your thoughts fly right out of your head like they're running a race. The whole point of having the gift of mind manipulation is that people don't realize it's happening."

My face reddens. "I know."

"Nothing to be embarrassed about, Hallie. You have a powerful gift. It will take you years to master all the gifts you have acquired. Come see me next week, and we'll set up some one-on-one time."

"Yes, ma'am. Is that all, Lady Jennica?" I look at the clock. "I have two minutes to get to my next class."

"Yes, yes," she says, pushing my back lightly to help me out the door. Then she says, "Hallie."

I turn around in the doorway. "Yes, ma'am?"

"How's Ivy holding up? She looks great, but you know . . ." There's a sadness in Lady Jennica's eyes that doesn't make sense.

"Um, Ivy's fine, I guess."

"Well, I know she's better now that she's with you."

"What are you talking about?" My voice is wispy, as if my lungs are hoarding the oxygen to deal with whatever comes next.

Lady Jennica's eyes squint, and she chooses her words with surgical care, a short pause between each word.

"You . . . don't . . ."

"I don't what?"

"It's nothing," she says, a fake smile growing on her face. Her eyes are still sad, troubled.

"Is there something wrong with Ivy? Is she okay?" As I say the words, my throat tightens.

Lady Jennica puts a hand on my arm. "Talk to Ivy."

I open my mouth to push her for more information, but she practically pushes me out the door. "You better get going," Lady Jennica says. "I'll see you tomorrow."

I just nod and walk numbly to my next class.

Six

I go through the rest of the day pretending I don't know something's wrong with Ivy. My mind has gone wild with possibilities.

Is it her grades? When mine came over the summer, I was terrified to open them. But my grades were good, and Ivy's smarter than I am.

Maybe she got a boyfriend over the summer and she's sad she had to leave him.

When I get to our room after our last class, I'm still trying to decide what to say.

Ivy takes one look at me and frowns. "Who died?"

Died? Did someone *die*? "You tell me," I say.

"What?" she asks. I can tell she's genuinely confused. She sits down next to me on my bed. "What's wrong?"

"Nothing," I say.

"Really? You're trying to lie to *me*? About your feelings?"

I smile back at my best friend. She knows me way too well to buy a lame answer like "nothing."

"Spill it," she says.

"Lady Jennica asked me something weird today."

"Oh yeah? What's that?"

"She asked if I'd had any trouble with my gifts over the summer. She seemed surprised I hadn't."

"What do you mean? You didn't play with your magic this summer at all?"

"Am I the only girl who actually followed the rules?"

Ivy smiles at me. "You're too good to be a witch. Especially one with black magic gifts."

"Don't remind me."

Black magic. Of all the girls at Dowling, I am the least likely to use black magic. As one of the few witches with the gift of inheritance, I am an inherently "black" witch.

Miss A would call it fate. Dad would call it ironic. I call it bad luck.

"That's all she wanted?" Ivy asks.

My mind snaps back to my conversation with Lady Jennica. "That was most of it."

"What else? Did she ask you about Kendall?"

"No," I say. I take a deep breath, swallow hard. *Say it!* "She asked me about you."

Ivy looks confused, and a quick flutter of hope blinks inside my belly. Maybe Lady Jennica was wrong. Maybe Ivy's fine and someone else is in trouble. Or dead.

"Why?"

"She wanted to make sure you were okay. She said you were probably better now that you're here with me."

I look straight into Ivy's eyes. "What's going on?"

Tears fill her eyes and she cries, so quietly, I can barely hear her. But the tears roll down her face, and she swipes at them angrily.

"Please tell me what's wrong, Ivy. I'm kinda freaking out right now."

I'm surprised when my own tears surface. I've never been a sympathy crier, but I've also never had a friend like Ivy.

"It's my parents," she says between swipes. "They're getting divorced." Her voice chokes on the last word. My heart breaks for her. I want to hug her, tell her it's going to be all right. But I don't know if things will be okay.

"I'm sorry," I whisper. It's the truest thing I can say.

She shrugs. "It's okay. I shouldn't be surprised. They haven't gotten along for a while. I just thought—" She stops midsentence, her voice catching on unshed tears.

I don't need the gift of empathy to feel her pain. I hold her hand and squeeze. "You should have told me."

Ivy shakes her head. "No sense ruining your summer too."

Her thoughtfulness is one of my favorite things about her. "Well, now I know and we're back at Dowling. You know I'm here for you, right?"

"I know," she says, a sad smile on her face. She takes a deep breath, stands up and goes to the sink in the bathroom. She washes her face and comes back out. Her face is still pink, but she looks good. She taps the watch on her wrist. "Dinnertime. I was going to check my e-mail, but that will have to wait."

I put a hand over my empty rumbling stomach. "Perfect timing."

We walk to the dining room and take our seats. The blessing is said, and plates are served. Mine last, again. Of course. Just as we begin eating, the headmistress taps a fork to her crystal water glass. The *ting, ting, ting* stops conversation, and silence falls through the room.

"Dowling sisters," she begins, her smile deceptively warm. "This is a very special year at Dowling."

I look at the girls around the table. They all look as confused as me.

The headmistress laughs quietly. She loves knowing more than everyone else in the room. Just like her daughter.

"This year Dowling will host Samhain, the Third Harvest celebration."

"Samhain?" I mouth the word to Ivy, who shrugs. "Third Harvest" triggers a small memory from one of our History of Witchcraft classes, but I don't recall the term "Samhain." And I sure don't remember the significance of the Third Harvest.

"It is a tremendous honor to be selected for this special event. We will invite former Dowling students as well as our brother school, Riley. Other covens will be invited to join as well."

You can practically feel the air being sucked out of the room when everyone gasps. The Riley boys are coming? My nerves go from cool to chaotic. Talking to Cody over e-mail is one thing. . . . Seeing him again in person is another.

I stretch to see Kendall and Zena at the front of the table, but they're facing the headmistress. I can imagine their faces are set in entitled smugness. They've probably known about this for months. There really should be a rule about the headmistress sharing information with her vile daughter. Even after her daughter cast a spell that nearly killed me, the headmistress has never checked on me or apologized for her daughter's behavior.

I look to Ivy, then Dru and Jo. They're as surprised as me, but they seem infinitely more excited.

"Did you hear that?" Ivy whispers loudly. Too loudly. Other girls at the table turn to shush her. Ivy rolls her eyes and leans closer to me. "You know what this means? You get to see Cody again."

My hammering head nods. "Uh-huh."

"Hello," she says, shaking my arm as if I'm asleep and she's trying to wake me. "That's *good* news."

I should be happy. Really happy. But I'm too nervous— too nauseous—to find happiness. How can I be excited and terrified at the same time?

"Why do you look like you're going to puke?" Ivy forces my eyes to lock onto hers. "You okay?"

Pull yourself together, Hallie. Deep breath. And another. Now . . . talk.

"Yeah, fine. I think I'm just really tired."

Ivy doesn't believe me, but she drops it.

I don't listen to the rest of the headmistress's announcement. Certain words penetrate my obsessive thinking.

"Dance . . . booths . . . crafts . . . contests . . . Riley."

I need air. And water. I need to think. I need air and water and space to think.

She's still talking when I turn to Ivy. "I'm going to step out for just a second."

I walk out of the room, prepared to face the consequences of leaving without permission. In the middle of the headmistress's announcement, no less. I'm sure I broke at least 329 rules.

When I'm safely outside the dining room doors, I walk to the entrance foyer.

Breathe.

I stop at the huge framed pictures and look at the image of Dannabelle Grimm, the last witch at Dowling with the gift of inheritance. Until me. I've been drawn to

Dannabelle since the first day I saw the picture, and even now, looking at her picture, I feel connected to her.

Dannabelle's eyes sparkle with mischief, and I envy her. I envy her confidence. Miss A tells me I'll get there one day, but I don't see how. In a million years I could never be like Dannabelle. I really think the gift of inheritance is wasted on me.

"Don't be silly," a voice says behind me.

I spin, breath held. The headmistress. I *really* have to watch what I'm thinking.

She laughs. "You'll learn how to control that, too," she says.

I nod, unconvinced.

"I saw you leave during my announcement. Is everything okay?" she asks.

"F-forgive me, Headmistress," I stammer. "I wasn't feeling well."

The headmistress looks at the image of Dannabelle behind me. "She's quite a legacy to follow."

Deep sigh. "You're telling me."

"The gift of inheritance comes with great responsibility, Hallie."

Her voice is stern, almost accusatory, contradicting the smile glued to her face.

Is that a question? Do I reply? I finally manage to say, "Yes, ma'am."

Awkward silence hangs between us.

"Controlling your gift will require considerably more time and practice than for other gifts. In fact, I'd say you will carry the heaviest out-of-classroom work."

This isn't news to me. "Miss A has prepared me for that."

"I would hate to see you fall behind because you're distracted."

"I am not easily distracted, Headmistress."

She smiles coldly. "I have noticed, Hallie. In fact, I admire your tenacity."

Somehow the words coming out of her mouth don't feel like a compliment.

"Thank you," I say anyway.

"The point I'm trying to make," the headmistress says, same plastic smile on her face, "Is that I hope you will be careful about committing yourself to activities, or people, outside of school. Particularly boys."

Is this about Cody? "No worries, ma'am. I don't antici-pate that being a problem for me."

"That's so good to hear," she says, putting her hand on my shoulder. "If you were to be distracted . . ." Her eyes are dark and sharp and scary. "Well, I suppose I should be going. There's much to plan for our celebration."

Before I can say good-bye, she's gone, the scent of ginger lingering where she stood.

Girls begin filling the hallway, dinner done. I watch each girl pass, wishing I had the same excited smile on my face that they do.

But I can't smile. I can't.

It's impossible to smile when the most powerful per-son in your life threatens you.

Seven

I don't sleep a full minute that night, and climb out of bed exhausted. I didn't tell Ivy what had happened with the headmistress. She'd insist I tell Miss A. And for now I like pretending it didn't happen.

I reach for my glasses and sit up in bed. The room is still dark. I always get up earlier than Ivy. I get up earlier than most people, actually. I've always been a morning girl.

I lean my head back against the wall and close my eyes, remembering my conversation with the head-mistress yesterday. There's so much I don't know, don't understand. But those who know—like Lady Rose and Lady Jennica—would never talk to me about the head-mistress. I have to figure out how to deal with her on my own.

I walk to the bathroom, flip on the light, and scream.

I shove my glasses onto my face, but I can't see anything. Everything's blurry, and my eyes hurt. I yank the glasses off and can see perfectly. But I'm *not* seeing perfectly, because the person in the mirror has bright blue eyes.

And mine are brown. Boring, basic, blah brown.

Bang, bang, bang. "Hal? You okay?"

"Hold on," I say, my voice more panicked than I intend.

I look back into the mirror. The blue eyes are still there. I lean closer. They aren't just blue; they're *blue*. I've never seen such a brilliant blue in my life.

"Hal," Ivy says, "open up."

I look at the glasses in my hand and realize I don't need them. I can see perfectly without them. For the first time since first grade, I can see perfectly. No glasses. No contacts.

"You're scaring me. I'm going to get Miss A."

Ivy's voice finally sinks in. I put a shaky hand on the bathroom door and turn the handle, prepare myself for her reaction.

Before I open the door, I warn her. "Don't freak out."

"Huh?"

"Don't go crazy on me. Okay?"

She shoves the door open, gets a good look at me, and then steps back. "What in Saffra's name—"

I hold up my glasses. "I don't even need these. I can see, as clear as day."

"Did you do this? Cast some sort of spell on yourself? Did you dream about it?"

"No, no," I say, shaking my head. "I just went to sleep like normal, woke up like normal, and then this."

"This is like last year . . . ," Ivy says, her voice trailing off.

"I was thinking the same thing."

Last year Kendall attempted to put a spell on us that would make us the ugliest girls in the coven. Kendall has the gift of transformation. So do I, actually. It's one of the gifts I inherited last year, and it's how Kendall got the forked tongue.

When Kendall and Zena put that spell on us, we woke up gorgeous. As in runway-ready rock-star stunning. And it stuck. We never changed back to our normal selves. Kendall was furious to learn she's a white witch, which means she's incapable of casting black magic spells, no matter how many times she tries.

"Think she did this?" Ivy asks what I'm thinking.

"Has to be," I say. "Who else could it be?"

Ivy leans closer to examine my eyes. "It's like they're lit or something. They're so . . . bright."

"I've got an idea," I say, grabbing her hand. I put on my robe and toss her her robe from the back of the bathroom door. "Put this on. We're going to see Miss A."

At six in the morning Dowling is silent. But I know Miss A is up. I don't think she sleeps a whole lot. We walk to the opposite end of the hallway, where Miss A's room is. We tap on her door lightly, so as not to wake girls in other rooms. Especially not Kendall and Zena, who are directly across from her.

She opens the door and stands proudly in a fluffy bright-pink-and-black-zebra-print robe. Rollers are tightly pinned all over her head. And her face is makeup free, which makes her look a lot different. So different, I probably wouldn't recognize her walking down the street. But there's something "real" about her like this. I think I like it.

"What in heaven's name are you two girls doing here?" she asks.

Then she looks at me, and slaps a hand over her gaping mouth. "Come in," she says, pulling us inside and looking down the hallway before closing the door gingerly.

She stands with her back to the door and smiles. "Hallie, you are a surprise a second, I tell you."

I show her the glasses in my hand. "No glasses. And no contacts. And I can still see everything."

Miss A plops down in her oversize well-worn recliner. "How'd you make that happen? Did you cast a spell on yourself?" She laughs, her eyes remembering something from years past. "Oh my, my, my, we have seen that happen plenty of times."

I shake my head. "No. I didn't do anything. Just went to bed like normal, then woke up like this."

"Hmm," Miss A says. "Reckon it could be the dynamic duo across the hall?"

Ivy nods, her head bobbing in quick, almost involuntary motion. "Yes, yes. That's what I think."

"Well, let's think about that," Miss A says. "Why would Kendall cast a spell like that on you again? Last time she did it, it backfired."

Ivy crosses her arms. "Those two think they know more than anyone else in the building. Zena probably convinced Kendall she should push the white magic aside and cast dark spells."

I hadn't thought that far along, but I bet Ivy's right. Miss A agrees too, nodding.

"So now what?" I ask. "Do we report the spell?"

"That's entirely your decision, Hallie. Dowling has a strict rule about casting spells before they've been taught to you. My guess is the complaint would 'get lost.'" She makes air quotes.

And I definitely don't want to be a rat.

"If I were you," Ivy says, "I'd make sure they saw your eyes first thing this morning. Let them stew on the fact that they can't cast spells to save their pitiful, materialist lives."

"And that?" I tell Ivy. "That's why you're my best friend."

At breakfast, Dru and Jo and Ivy are still fascinated with my eyes. I am too, I guess. I don't get to see them like they do.

"It's like they . . . I don't know. Glow or something." Dru tilts her head to one side, then to the other.

"That's it!" Jo slaps her hand on the table. "I know what you look like."

I brace myself for something awful.

"Snow White!"

Ivy pulls back so she can get a good look at me. "You know what? You're right. Dark hair, pale skin, blue eyes."

"Only things missing are the dwarves," Dru says, then breaks into hysterics.

"Funny," I say, unable to hide my smile. "You're a regular comedian."

Ivy grasps my wrist. "There they are."

I don't have to turn around to know she means Kendall and Zena. We watch them go through the buffet line, get their drinks, then sit down.

"Dang it," Dru says. "They didn't even look over here."

"It's okay," I say. I take a long swig of my orange juice, then stand. "I'll be right back."

Every step I take closer to Kendall and Zena, my heart rate jumps even higher. I look back at my table and see my friends staring at me in shock. Like I'm walking through the room naked. And I won't lie. . . . It kind of feels like that. Because the closer I get to their table, the more people are watching me. The feud between Kendall and me is epic and definitely not a secret.

My hands go cold and clammy, and I can feel the red

spots spreading across my chest. Thankfully, no one will see them because I'm wearing my sweater.

Can't turn back now.

I get closer, closer, closer.

Two more steps and I'm standing directly in front of Kendall. She looks up, mouth poised to hurl a well-rehearsed insult at me.

But she doesn't insult me.

She doesn't do anything at all.

The color drains from her face, and I know I've got her.

I put my hands on the table, lean in close so my face is just a foot away from hers. I blink a few times, just to be sure she sees them, then whisper, "Surprise."

Eight

When we walk into Lady Rose's room, I'm flying high. I have never been so satisfied with myself. And Kendall's stupefied face was like the best gift I've ever received.

"I can't believe you did that," Ivy says. "I can't believe you had the nerve."

"Me either. But, darn, it felt good."

The room goes quiet when Lady Rose walks in. She teaches the Elements of Witchcraft class. It's where we learn the real witch stuff about our gifts and spells. That kind of thing. Lady Rose isn't as hip as Lady Jennica, but she's cool in her own way. After all, she's the one who teaches us magic. It'd be impossible to hate the class, or her.

"Well, ladies, here we are. Year two here at Dowling. Did everyone sleep okay?"

The group nods and groans at the same time, making her smile.

"Well, maybe I can help wake you up. Let's talk about our goals this year."

With a clap of her hands, the room goes dark and the projector screen lights up with a PowerPoint titled "Crafter Goals."

"Our first goal," she says as the PowerPoint goes to a new slide, "is what I like to call 'fine-tuning' our gifts. We'll learn how to better manage our skills. When that happens, the lights will stay on and the blinds will catch a break in Lady Jennica's room."

Everyone laughs, and some girls blush, knowing they're to blame for the now broken window blinds in our history class.

A new slide comes on.

Learn new spells.

Some girls clap, and others shout "Yeah!" out loud. This is what we've all been waiting for. We have our gifts, and that's cool—supercool, actually. But when you learn spells, you can actually make things happen intentionally. And witches can do some pretty cool things when they know what they're doing.

"That's always a crowd-pleaser," Lady Rose says with a smile. "Let me prepare you, girls. We will begin with small spells. Only when I'm convinced you've mastered those responsibly will we move on. And we will all move at the same pace. It's an all-for-one kind of thing."

Kendall looks at Zena, like she's seeking affirmation that the rules don't apply to them. Zena shrugs, but I don't know what that means. What I *do* know is that neither Zena nor Kendall care for rules. It's not in their nature to wait for the group.

"There are no exceptions to this rule," Lady Rose says. "Every single one of you will master the basics before any of us move on." She looks at Zena pointedly, but Zena is looking in her purse for something. Probably some evil magic dust.

A girl in the back of the room raises her hand, and our teacher nods to her. "Is it hard to learn spells?"

Lady Rose thinks about this a moment. "That's a great question."

Ivy looks behind us to see who asked the question. She turns back to me and shrugs. "I don't know her," she whispers.

I sneak a look back and recognize her as one of the girls constantly chasing after Kendall and Zena, willing to do almost anything to be part of their group. I've never quite understood how Kendall always managed to stay so popular. I used to think it was because she was pretty and girls thought being with her made them pretty too, but now I just think some girls are delusional. Like this girl.

I think her name is Cassie. She sits up straight next to another familiar girl I can't name. You'd think I'd know more people after being here a year. But I was so wrapped up in my insane world last year that I didn't have time to make many friends.

"Are spells hard to learn?" Lady Rose says. "Well, I'll tell you this much. Casting a spell correctly requires a great deal of focus. Your mind must be like a laser, narrowing in on the smallest details of the spell. You also have to learn the elements that go with spells, so that takes some practice. And you have to remember that you won't always get it right the first time."

Lady Rose looks at Kendall and Zena again. Her face is somber, but the effect is totally lost on those two girls. "If you attempt to cast a spell before you're ready," she says, "it can have disastrous results."

When she looks at me and gives me the tiniest little grin, I know she's talking about the spell they put on me last year. Lady Rose is one of the only teachers who isn't afraid of the headmistress. Most of our teachers let Zena do what she wants, and since Kendall is her best friend, that extends to her as well.

"Before we can get started on spells, we have to be fully in tune with our minds."

This time last year, that would have sounded like a bunch of nonsense, but now it sounds logical. I know what she means. Witchcraft is entirely in the head. I've found that most things are.

"We'll start by mastering dream recall," she says, and a new slide clicks on. A photo of stars and mist and a full moon fills the screen. "Dream recall is exactly what it sounds like. It's training your brain to remember your dreams. Can anyone guess why we'd want to know what we dream about?"

Dru raises her hand, and Lady Rose nods in her direction.

"My mother always says that dreams are important because they reflect deep thoughts you ignore when you're awake," Dru says.

"She's right," Lady Rose says. "Dreams always have meaning. Believe it or not, you can learn to recall almost all your dreams. I'll teach you some simple techniques to help you start remembering dreams within the first or second night of practice. It's sort of like self-hypnosis in a way. You are simply making suggestions to your mind before you are completely asleep. This state of mind is called the borderline sleep level. It is when your brain is most likely to absorb the suggestions."

Lady Rose claps her hands, and just enough lights come on for us to see. "Girls, get your notebooks out. You need to take some notes."

The room rustles with activity. Even Zena and Kendall grab their notebooks, and I think it may be the first time I've seen them actually take notes.

"Starting tonight I want you to follow these steps. They sound so simple. Too simple, really. But it works, girls. I promise. I do this every night."

She writes on the board: *1) Preparing your mind for rest.*

"When you are preparing for bed, it's important to get your body as relaxed as you can. You can meditate to clear your mind, so that you are ready for the next step. Make sure you have a notepad and pen beside your bed."

She gives us time to write, then continues. She returns to the board and writes: 2) *Programming.*

"This is the most important part. When you get to that borderline sleep level, which is right before you are completely asleep, you must tell yourself over and over again that you will remember all your dreams and you will wake up after each dream and write it down. You can also ask to dream about something important. If you're struggling with an important decision, ask for Saffra's help while you sleep."

Ivy looks at me like, *This sounds crazy,* and I agree with her. But it still sounds pretty cool.

"Next," she says, writing on the board again, "is a critical part of the process."

3) *Taking Notes.*

"If you successfully wake up after each dream, then you must write down everything you can remember in detail. Write down whether the dream was in color or black and white. This is why you need to keep a pen and pad next to the bed. Make sure not to put them in the bed with you. You don't want to end up stabbing yourself with the pen in your sleep." Everyone giggles. "Then you must try to go right back to sleep."

It's kind of creepy, but I can't wait to try this, to see if it really works.

She writes one last note on the board. *4) Reviewing the Night.*

"You'll be amazed how many dreams you actually have each night. I usually find that I have ten to fifteen dreams a night; sometimes more."

Someone behind me says, "There are some nights when I don't have any dreams. What do I do on those nights?"

"Everyone dreams several times a night. They just don't know they do until they try something like this. Make special note of dreams in full-blown color. You'll want to reference them once we are further along in the process."

The bell rings, and everyone throws their notebooks and pens into their bags as Lady Rose reminds us to bring our dream journals to class tomorrow.

Just as I'm leaving the room, someone pulls at my sleeve. I turn to see Lady Rose, whose face is smiling, but it's not a real smile and fails to reach her eyes.

She looks at Ivy waiting for me at the door. "Ivy, I need Hallie for just a second."

Ivy nods, leaving me behind for the second day in a row.

"Is something wrong, Lady Rose?" I ask once the class is cleared.

She shakes her head, but her eyes are sad. Worried. "How is this year shaping up so far?"

"Good," I tell her. "Really good, actually."

"I know you had problems with Kendall last year. Is that any better?"

I shake my head. "Things with Kendall will never be easy. But at least we aren't roommates."

I'm about to point out my new blue eyes. But she looks distracted, so I don't say anything.

"I'm sure," Lady Rose says, her face unchanged. "I just . . ."

I don't fill the silence, and let her finish her thought.

"You know this year will be different."

I nod at her. "It already is."

Lady Rose closes her eyes.

"What are you trying to say, Lady Rose?"

"I'm probably just being overprotective. I've never had a student with your gift. You are a very talented and unique young witch. There are powerful people at Dowling who might . . ."

Before she finishes her thought, girls begin entering her room for the next class.

Lady Rose puts her hand on my arm. "Come see me if you need anything."

I look at her, wishing I could ask her questions. I have so many. But the room is crowding fast, and I have to get to my next class.

I smile, an empty, halfhearted smile. "Yes, ma'am. See you tomorrow."

I leave the room, but the chill of her words stays with me for hours.

Nine

Seven thirty. Two hours till lights out.

I have genealogy research that needs my attention, but I'm temporarily trapped in my room. Jo and Dru said they had some juicy news to share, so of course they came over right after dinner.

I'm at my desk, checking e-mail while they giggle and gossip behind me. Most of my e-mail is junk. But one sender catches my attention. Cody.

I glance over my shoulder to see if anyone is looking, but they're too busy talking about the upcoming celebration to notice. The cursor hovers over his name, but I don't click on it. Not yet. I minimize my screen, turn around in my chair and straddle it backward.

I jump into the conversation when there's a break.

"So, what's the gossip we just had to hear tonight?"

Jo and Dru share a look.

"Tell us!" Ivy says.

Dru giggles. "Okay. So, we were in the library today, working on research. There were a lot of people in there. I've never seen the library so crowded. Have either one of you started your research?"

"Focus, Dru," I say. "Gossip first. School second."

Wait. Did those words come out of my mouth? I've always said school trumps everything. Even gossip. And especially boys.

"Right," she says, giving Jo another look. My nerves prickle. This must be really good.

"We're working, and I started hearing someone's conversation," Jo says. How Jo can hear some conversations but tune out others is a mystery to me.

"You're so lucky," Ivy says. She's exasperated that her gift isn't stealthier.

Jo shakes her head. "Hardly."

"Anyway . . . ," I say.

"Anyway," Jo continues. "I realize it's Kendall and Zena."

My stomach clenches. Nothing good comes from those two.

"What were they talking about?" Ivy asks. "Their next plan to take over the world?"

Dru is too antsy to let Jo finish. "It was about Cody."

Everyone in the room freezes.

"What about him?" I ask in my best why-should-I-care voice.

"It turns out your boyfriend—" Dru says.

"He is *not* my boyfriend." I'm so emphatic, spit shoots from my lips.

"Relax, Hallie," Ivy says.

Jo finishes telling us about the conversation she overheard. "Zena said Cody is in line to be the next High Priest of Riley."

Stunned silence.

Until finally Ivy says, "Oh. My. Gosh."

"Did they say anything else?" I ask, my voice strained. Why did I have to get involved with *this* guy? Of course he's going to be the next High Priest. I finally let myself like someone, and he's untouchable. He'll have his pick of any girl.

"Just that he'd take over when he turns twenty-one. I couldn't hear the whole thing. There were too many people in there, and I had trouble picking out their voices after a while."

"Hallie, do you know what this means?" Ivy asks.

"It means nothing," I say. I'm dying to read Cody's e-mail now. "It's just gossip. I don't even know what a High Priest does. Or a High Priestess for that matter. If Zena said it, I refuse to believe it."

They look at me like I'm crazy. And I probably am. But I don't want to consider things like Cody being a High Priest and what that means for me.

I cross my arms in defense. "Really. Since when do we trust a single word that comes out of Zena Fallon's mouth?"

No one has a decent comeback. "Exactly," I say. "Since never. It's just Zena trying to make herself look important. Zena cares about one thing. One person. And absolutely nothing else. Not even Kendall."

"I don't know," Jo says. "I mean, what if she's right?"

"What if she is?" I ask. "It changes nothing. Not for the four of us and not for me and Cody."

"Don't you want to know if the guy you're crushing on is Riley royalty?"

"Royalty? Let's save the melodrama for Kendall and Zena."

What would Kendall and Co. say if they knew I talked to Cody all summer? And not just once or twice but every day? Then they'd really be excited about this gossip.

There's a tap at the door before Miss A walks in. "Howdy-ho! How are my favorite girls doing?"

My anxiety weakens just by having her here. It's like she knows I need her.

Then I look at her and she winks. Of course she knows. She practically lives in my head.

"I decided to have an impromptu meeting to discuss our contribution to the Third Harvest celebration. Let's meet in the Crafter Chamber. End of the hall. Last door on the right. Be there in fifteen minutes."

In a snap she has bustled out of our room and headed to the next.

"Wonder what kind of booth we're going to have," Ivy says. "I hope it isn't something lame like a dunking booth."

"Maybe we could have a kissing booth," Dru says with a wink. "Put Hallie in that baby and Cody will never leave."

"And Dowling would get rich!" Jo is the last to join in, and when she does, we all laugh. But my heart isn't totally in it. I need to read Cody's e-mail, but I can't with my friends sitting right here. And I definitely don't want them to know about it.

I take one last look at my laptop before leaving the room.

⭑   ⭑   ⭑   ⭑   ⭑

The Crafter Chamber is nicer than the Seeker Sanctum. It has plush seats and sofas instead of folding chairs, and the room is lit by candles hanging from the ceiling. It's the perfect temperature. Perfect everything. Instead of being in rows, the chairs and sofas are arranged in a circle.

"Very cool," Ivy says.

"And I'm *very* glad we got here first," I add.

Seating is first-come, first-serve, and where you sit in the first meeting is where you wind up sitting all year. It's not a rule; it's just the way it is.

"Where do we want to sit?" Dru asks.

We look around the room, and all our eyes settle on the same little nook close to the left of Miss A's podium. Two chairs and a love seat. It even has a table in the center.

"That's where," I say. We make quick work of picking out our places—Jo and Dru on the love seat, Ivy and me in chairs.

As girls arrive, they move furniture around to fit their groups, and everyone seems excited about the new room.

Miss A rings the chimes sitting on her podium. The room is silent almost instantly. Miss A may not be as harsh and refined as the other dorm moms, but she is every bit as strict.

"Advancing at Dowling has its perks, does it not?" she asks.

Excited voices and a few claps answer.

"It's time to begin. Crafters, prepare your minds."

As we close our eyes in anticipation of Miss A's blessing, the door opens and hits the wall with a loud *thud*.

Everyone's head shoots up to see Kendall and Zena entering. According to the clock over the door, they're exactly four minutes late.

Miss A snaps her fingers at them. "Sit right here. In front of me," she orders.

I have to bite my lip to keep from laughing, as do most of the other girls in the room.

Zena doesn't move, challenging Miss A. "Crafters get to choose where they sit."

Her know-it-all voice makes me angry. I can hardly stand to hear it.

Miss A snaps her fingers again, willing the girls forward. "You lost that right when you chose to be late. Now sit down. We don't have time to waste."

Ten

"Samhain is going to be a stellar event, girls. We are so fortunate to host it. Our contribution has to be wicked good." Miss A laughs at her clever wording. "We have a few choices that we need to discuss, then vote on. The celebration is on Halloween, of course, as all Third Harvest celebrations are."

"What kind of things can we do?" A girl in the back of the room named Missy asks the question. We have all the same classes but don't really know each other. Miss A claps her hands in front of her chest. "Well, it's been a while since we've had one of these. I was just a teenager at the last celebration Dowling hosted. It was a joint party celebrating the Third Harvest and the 'retirement' of a former headmistress, Janice Seaver. She was the headmistress before Fallon and McCarty. Each head-mistress brings their own . . . style."

I can hardly imagine Dowling without Headmistress Fallon at the helm. I wonder if things were a lot different without her around.

"Things were different back then," Miss A says, with a wink to me. "Not better or worse, just . . . different." A look of sadness crosses her face, and then—poof—it's gone.

She launches into a frenzied list of all the ideas she's come up with.

Kissing booth (cheek only, of course). Lame.

Face painting. Um, no. We aren't six.

"What can we do that guys will like too?" Ivy asks in our circle.

"What about tattoos?" I ask loudly enough for the other girls to hear. "We'd use washable paint."

The room goes silent. Then a low hum begins to fill the air.

Miss A watches the excitement grow, ignoring Zena and Kendall, who are sitting with their arms crossed in defiance. Even if they love the idea, they'll never admit it.

Missy, from the back of the room, speaks up again.

"We could come up with symbols for each gift, and that could be the tattoo you receive."

Jo jumps to her feet. "I can do that! I love to draw."

Miss A holds up her hands. "All right, girls. Sounds like we have a solid idea. Let's take a vote."

She waits for the room to quiet, which takes a few minutes. My tattoo idea makes everyone forget how tired they are, how much homework remains undone, how homesick they are.

"There are candles on the tables around you. Please take one."

I look at the table, and sure enough, there are four candles. Were these candles here earlier? I'm almost positive they weren't. But it's Dowling. Anything can happen here.

We each grab an unlit candle.

"If you would like to vote that we offer a tattoo booth, please light your candle."

I look at my friends for a clue about how to do that without matches or a lighter, but they're as confused as I am.

"My bad," Miss A says, giggling. She always tries to talk like the cool kids, as she says, but it always sounds silly. Why doesn't it sound that ridiculous when we say it?

"I forgot you don't know how to vote at Dowling. Feels like you girls have been here forever." She takes an unlit candle to the front of the room and holds it in front of her. "Hold your candle as I am. Then place your fingers on the wick and pull up quickly."

We follow her directions, and every candle in the room lights.

Dru gasps. "That's so cool."

Miss A watches us with the pride of a parent. "Very good. Now blow them out."

Again we do as she says, and the room falls dim.

"This time," she says, "you will only light your candle if you want to vote that we host a tattoo booth at Samhain."

I light my candle, as do most of the other girls in the room. Zena and Kendall, of course, keep their candles on the table. We don't have to count candles to know the tattoo booth is a winner.

"Well, congratulations, girls. We've had our first Crafter vote." Miss A is pleased with herself, and with us. "Next step is to determine who's in charge of what."

Miss A makes quick work of leading us in decisions about who will create the artwork, who will create the booth, who will buy the supplies. We're back in our room by nine, charged with excitement but exhausted.

"That was different," I say. I put my iPhone on the speakers and put on my favorite playlist. Katy Perry, Maroon 5, and Lorde.

"Did you see the looks on their faces?" Ivy asks.

"It was beautiful," I say.

Ivy yawns loudly, contorting her face into a funny expression.

"Did you notice how Miss A said 'retirement' today? Like it wasn't really a retirement?" I ask. "Did that seem weird to you?"

Ivy drops to her bed and curls up with a big pile of pillows. "Everything at Dowling is weird, Hallie."

"Yeah, but this is different. And then she got this sad look on her face. I don't know. I just think there's more to that story."

Ivy opens her eyes just a peek. "Yeah, I did notice that. What difference does it make?"

"Well, it has me thinking. Why did that Seaver woman leave? Seems to me that being a headmistress is a pretty easy job. And you get to live here for free. Doesn't sound too awful, if you ask me. Think she was old? Or maybe she did something wrong?"

Ivy opens her eyes completely and sits up lazily. She pulls her favorite pillow to her chest. "Leaving Dowling—the building—is one thing. Girls do that all the time. Leaving the coven altogether is another."

"Did your sister tell you that?"

Ivy's face is unreadable. There's something—maybe a lot of things—she's keeping to herself.

She smoothes the fuzz on the pillow, focusing way too hard on making each piece lie perfectly straight. "Ivy," I say. "You can tell me anything. You know that."

She held back the news of the divorce. Who knows what else is locked away in her head.

"Is it your parents?" I ask.

Ivy looks up at me, tears making her eyes sparkle. I move from my bed, sit next to her, put my arm around her, and sigh. "Talk to me. You'll feel better if you do, I promise."

Her voice is controlled. "When my sister left, she *left*. She didn't really graduate like I told you. She rejected her gifts and has never given time or money back to the coven."

"What? Why would she do that?" You learn early on at Dowling that even when you leave, you're still connected to the coven. You have obligations to Dowling forever. It's what keeps the coven going.

Ivy shrugs. "She was tired of being told what to do, what to wear, how to act, what kind of magic she was allowed to practice."

"Everyone has to deal with that," I say. "No one likes that part."

"She was in trouble all the time for not following the rules. When a Dowling girl rejects her gifts, it's considered a disgrace to the family. Usually, they just shun your entire family. Like you don't exist anymore."

My mouth drops open. "That seems so . . ."

"Severe? Harsh? Extreme?" Ivy supplies.

"Yeah. All of that."

We sit in silence a few minutes. Then I realize something. "If your family was shunned, how are you here?"

Ivy lets out a bitter, resentful laugh. "I'm the only one who can restore our family's name. I must stay at Dowling until I've completed every level, then fulfill all my duties to Dowling after I leave. And I also have to fulfill all of Linette's as well."

That burden must feel like she's carrying the Statue

of Liberty on her back. Up fifty flights of stairs. Barefoot.

I should know—I'm in the same boat. If I don't make it through Dowling, my family loses their Dowling heritage too.

I don't know what to say. Mom says that sometimes you don't need to say anything to make someone feel better. Just be there.

So that's what I do. I stay next to Ivy and don't ask her any more questions. Just stay still and show her I'm here for her.

And then I have a thought. "So maybe that's what happened to Seaver."

Ivy looks at me out of the corner of her eye. "Really?"

"I don't know. Maybe."

We don't talk about it anymore. But I know what we are both thinking.

What could a headmistress do to get herself kicked out of Dowling?

Eleven

Ivy grabs her favorite Hello Kitty pj's from the dresser, then checks her cell phone messages. "I'm going to take a shower."

My eyes dart to my laptop. This is my chance to read Cody's e-mail.

"Okay," I say. When she takes her time with the phone, I have to stop myself from shoving her into the bathroom faster so I can get to my e-mail.

She finally shuts the bathroom door, and when I hear the water turn on, I grab my laptop and open it. My e-mail is still open, and Cody's message is still there. My heart does some weird little jumping in my chest. Nerves.

I look at the subject line. *Samhain.* My fingers hover over the computer, not quite ready to open the e-mail.

I look at the bathroom door. Ivy takes quick showers. I don't have much time.

I double click the e-mail, and it opens.

```
To: halliecat@dowling.edu
From: codyray@rileyacademy.edu
Re: Samhain
Hi, Hallie. How are you? How has the
first week been? We've been busy with all
the normal stuff. Sorry I haven't e-mailed
you. We just got our laptops today.
The headmaster told us about the Third
Harvest celebration and that Dowling gets
to host it. That's kind of a big deal. We
get to go if all of our assignments are
turned in and we don't get into trouble.
But don't worry, I will be there. Anyway,
just wanted to say hi and that I'll see
you at the celebration.
Cody
```

My pulse pounds in my ears. I reread the e-mail. Cody will be at the celebration. Of course, I knew he would. He goes to Riley, and the Riley boys are coming. But I can't let myself get excited about any of it. Because I worry that my friends will know we've been talking all summer.

I worry that my friends will make a really big deal of it and be mad at me for not telling them sooner.

But mainly I worry that my clothes won't be right for the celebration.

Ivy's voice empties my mind of everything the second I hear her. "You got an e-mail from Cody?"

I try to hit the escape key on the laptop to close the e-mail. I'm too late. She's already seen it.

Ivy doesn't apologize for nearly scaring me to death. Or for being nosy. She grabs the laptop and pulls it closer to her.

"Hey," I complain. "You're getting the screen all wet."

She ignores me *and* the water spots she just put on my laptop screen.

Not cool.

She puts the laptop back, then squirts a mountain of mousse into her hand and runs it through her hair.

"So." Her voice is normal, but she's irritated. I can tell.

"So?" I ask. Playing it cool is the best way to go here. I think.

"So I'm not the only one keeping secrets."

"I'm not keeping any secrets. Just checking my e-mail."

Ivy gives me a *Yeah, right* look. "So is it, like, a date?"

"What?" I point at the e-mail still on my screen. "This?"

"Yes, Hallie Simon. That."

I give my best scoff and close the laptop's cover, put the computer back on my desk carefully. "Not even."

"Does Cody know that?"

"It's not like he asked me to go to the celebration with him."

"Well, duh," Ivy says, hiding behind the closet door as she changes. "He's coming *here*. Did you read the e-mail? He definitely wants to see you."

My face heats up when she says that.

"Okay. Now it's your turn to talk." Ivy sits on her bed, legs folded, hands in her lap, like we're in kindergarten and it's story time.

"There isn't much to tell," I say. It's a small half-truth. Not really a lie.

"How often did you talk to him this summer?" She points a stern finger at me. "Don't even think about lying."

"You can't tell a single person about this. Not even Dru and Jo."

She rolls her eyes. "Seriously? You think you have to say that?"

Deep breath. And another one.

"Spill it, Hal," Ivy says, snapping her fingers.

"We exchanged e-mail addresses at the dance last year," I begin. "I didn't think much of it at the time because we didn't even have Internet access. Then when I went home, I had six e-mails from Cody."

"Six?" Ivy's eyes go wide. "Nice! What'd the e-mails say?"

"Nothing special. Just 'What are you doing?' and 'Are you going on vacation this summer?' That kind of thing."

It feels good to tell Ivy about Cody. Keeping it inside has been harder than I realized. "And how often did you e-mail after that?" she asks.

I tell her how we e-mailed several times a day, how we told each other about our families, how we shared our newfound gifts with each other. "Mostly, though, it was just stupid stuff. Cartoons, funny YouTube videos."

Ivy tosses a pillow at me and it hits my face. "Doesn't sound stupid to me. Sounds pretty dang cool. But what do I know? I'm just an empath."

I throw the pillow back at her and change into an

oversize T-shirt. I don't even bother brushing my teeth. I just crawl into the sheets and grab my journal.

"Don't forget your dream journal," I tell Ivy.

Ivy holds the journal up. "Already on it. What are we supposed to do?"

"Tell yourself you want to remember your dreams. And think of something specific you want to dream about."

"That's a long list. Do I just pick one thing?"

"Lady Rose didn't say, but I guess so."

A few minutes of silence pass. "What do you want to dream about?" I ask Ivy.

"Can we tell each other? Or is it like the wish you make when you blow out your birthday candles and it only comes true if you don't say what you wished for?"

I laugh. "I'm pretty sure this isn't quite the same thing. But you can keep it a secret."

Ivy sighs and turns off the light. "I don't want to jinx it."

My eyes adjust to the darkness. As I turn to face the wall, Ivy does the same. The room's silent, but I know we are both doing lots of talking in our heads.

I sit up in bed, heart pounding so hard, I feel like it's actually hitting my ribs. The clock on my nightstand says it's four thirteen a.m. Why in the world am I awake?

Then I remember.

My dream.

I grab the journal from my nightstand and turn the lamp on. I throw a blanket over the lamp so it isn't so bright. Ivy doesn't move.

I take the pen and begin writing. I write fast, messily, afraid that I'll lose some little nugget of information if I don't go fast.

Cody.

Fire.

The headmistress.

Kendall.

"It's your destiny, Cody."

Then crying.

Fire. Fire.

I look at Ivy, sleeping so silently.

Maybe my dream is just . . . just a dream. But Lady Rose's words echo in my head. *Dreams always have meaning.*

I look back at my journal and fill in a lingering image.

Candles. But that isn't where the fire's coming from.

Ivy turns over in bed. "You okay?"

"I'm fine," I whisper. I turn off the lamp and put the journal on my desk. But my eyes stay open until dawn.

Twelve

I can't get the dream out of my head. Even when Cody e-mails me again, asking about what our booth will be at Samhain, images from my dream linger. I want to tell him about the dream, but I don't even understand it myself.

I tell Cody he'll have to wait until the celebration to find out because the Crafters have decided to keep it a secret.

We're sitting in the dining room, finishing lunch, when Missy stops at our seats. "Hey, Jo," she says, "Can I sit here with you? I wanted to show you some of my drawings."

Jo was elected to oversee the creation of the tattoos for each gift. She's a great artist, but she can't draw them all and teach us how to draw them all by herself, so she asked for some help, and Missy was the first to offer. They look over the drawings, and it's obvious Jo approves.

"Look, Ivy," says Jo, passing a sheet of paper to her. "This will be yours."

I look at the paper as Ivy inspects it.

Ivy must look as confused as I feel, because Missy explains what it means. "The two *Y*s represent hands holding, or crossing spirits. It's what happens when you feel what others feel."

Ivy hands the paper back. "Looks great. Thanks, Missy."

"Have you done mine?" Dru asks.

"Or mine?" I ask.

Jo shakes her head. "Not yet. There are a lot of symbols to create. But when I get them done, I'll show you."

I give her a thumbs-up. The design is really the farthest thing from my mind. Right now I can only think about Cody, what my dream could mean, and how I can figure it out.

We're in Lady Rose's class, and I'm clutching my dream journal. I've been worried Ivy would ask to look at it.

But I haven't asked her, and she hasn't asked me.

"Good afternoon," Lady Rose says. The door closes with a snap of her fingers, and the candles on a long white table illuminate.

"I trust everyone kept their dream journal last night. Remember that is personal information. Never feel obligated to share your dreams with another. The purpose of the exercise is to practice our awareness. We have incredible power over our thoughts if we'll just learn how to control them. Meditating on what you want to dream about is a small step in harnessing that control."

The dream journal is on my desk, my hands still tightly wrapped around it. I really don't want to know what my dream meant, but I can't *not* find out.

"Today," Lady Rose says, "we will learn our first spell. I always like to start with something simple but meaningful. Today you'll learn a spell to help you with studying."

Everyone in the room is whispering things like "Awesome" and "Thank Saffra!"

She waits for the class to quiet down before she continues. "I was hoping you'd feel that way. Please get out your Book of Shadows and a pen."

I grab the Book of Shadows from my bag and put my dream journal in its place. I search my bag for a pen but can only find pencils and highlighters. I almost ask Dru to make one appear for me, but our teacher doesn't like gratuitous use of our gifts.

I raise my hand. "Lady Rose, may I borrow a pen?"

She walks to me, smiling. "Here you go," she says.

The pen doesn't fit right in my hand. It's different. And old. Like, really old. It's made of some sort of marble, and it has a metal triangle at the bottom, where the ink comes out. You might know I'd get a funky pen for the very first spell I get to add to my great-great-grandmother's Book of Shadows. Every student inherits a Book of Shadows from her most recent witch ancestor, and I found my book in the attic back home. Considering it's over a hundred years old, it's in pretty good shape. A few worn edges, and the paper is kind of brittle. But it's durable, and Miss A promises me it will last a lifetime.

Lady Rose stands behind the long table. "At the top of the first clean page, please write 'Study Spell.'"

The swish of pens across paper breaks the silence. I struggle with the pen. Of all the days for me to forget mine.

"Now you need to list the ingredients."

Ingredients? Like a recipe?

"A spell is sort of like a recipe," she answers. "It has to be precise, and you have to follow certain steps. Here are your ingredients for this spell."

She points to the items on the table as she tells us what they are.

"First thing you need is a yellow candle. You can use white, but yellow is more powerful."

I write in my book. *Yellow candle. Better than white.*

"Next thing you need is something to carve symbols into the candle. I use a toothpick, but use whatever works for you." She holds up a toothpick, then lays it back on the table next to the candle.

Next she holds up a piece of paper and a pen. Her pen looks almost identical to the one she let me borrow. "You need a small piece of paper and a pen."

"Finally," she says, holding up a small glass dish, "you need a flameproof dish."

She gives everyone a few minutes to finish writing before she continues.

"Now, before I tell you how to conduct the spell, here's a warning."

Ivy leans over and whispers. "Pay attention to this."

I give her an eye roll, but she makes sense. As a black magic witch, almost everything I try to do goes wrong.

Lady Rose's voice goes stern. "This is not a spell to be recited in place of studying. It is to heighten your retention of what you learn and then study."

I make a note in my journal. *Still have to study.*

"Let's proceed, ladies. This spell works best when studying with classmates. You can, of course, do this on your own. But the more witches in the spell, the stronger it is."

Another note. *Practice with a circle of friends.*

"You can perform the spell where your study area is. The library, your room, anywhere you study is fine. Carve a symbol representative of academic success, such as a good grade or the rune for wisdom, into the candle."

"What's a rune?" Dru calls out. I'm glad she asked, because I've never heard that word either.

"I knew you'd ask," Lady Rose says. "Runes are a set of characters from ancient magic cultures. The rune for wisdom and insight is a sideways *V*. Most students remember it as the 'less than' sign you use in math when comparing numbers."

That's what I write in my book. *Rune for wisdom and insight—less than sign.* <

"After you've carved the symbol into the candle, sit before it for a moment to focus and center yourself. Then imagine the candle's light filling your head, making your mind clear, focused, alert."

I scramble to write what she said in my book, but my pen is funky and makes the ink come out in little gobs, and the whole page looks messy. And that's a problem, because I don't do messy.

"Now that you're focused, and the candle has been carved, you're ready to chant the incantation. Remember that chanting is quiet, private. It is not to be said loudly or in anger. Clear minds are critical to good spell casting."

As she tells us the incantation, I write it down. She makes us repeat it with her several times, and even in a room of twenty-eight girls, we hardly make any sound at all.

"Bright and lively is this flame.
I will my mind to be the same.
I'll be attentive as it burns.
Remembering everything I learn.
I'll focus well and study hard.
Success will be my due reward."

By the time we've chanted the incantation several times, I feel like I've been hypnotized. Like I just woke up from a long rainy-day nap.

"After the incantation, you will draw the rune for disordered thoughts on the piece of paper. It's an easy symbol—a star. Catch the paper on fire with the candle's flame and put it into the flameproof dish. As it burns to ashes, imagine the same thing happening to any distracting thoughts, allowing you to focus completely on your studies. Study within your circle, keeping the candle lit. When you are done studying, snuff out the candle and close your circle with a blessing. If the candle burns out, get a new one and redo the spell."

Ivy looks at me, eyes excited. "We are totally doing this tonight when we study for our math test."

We high-five. "It's a date."

Thirteen

"Got everything?" Ivy asks when I walk into our room. I hold up the bag that contains what we need for the studying spell. "Sometimes it pays to be the teacher's pet."

We put the candle on the floor between us, along with our math books. We each open our Book of Shadows. I can hardly read what I wrote. "That pen Lady Rose loaned me was weird. Look at this. It's a mess. Think I can tear this page out and rewrite my notes?"

Ivy slaps a hand onto my open book. "No! Never tear a page out of that book."

"Okaaaay," I say, removing her hand slowly.

"Promise me you won't. Really, *really* bad things can happen."

"How do you know? Did Linette tell you that?"

"Promise me." Her voice is more serious, and I realize she isn't kidding.

I hold up two fingers. "Scout's honor."

Ivy lets out a huge sigh, like she just saved my life. Which only makes me more curious about what happens when a page is torn out of the Book of Shadows. Curiosity can be dangerous at Dowling.

"Should I turn off the lights?" I ask.

Ivy lights the candle with her fingertips like we learned in the Crafter meeting, then nods.

I flip the switch, and the yellow candle lights our room. The last bit of sun peeks through the blinds. It gets dark earlier and earlier this time of year. "We have an hour to study before dinner," Ivy says.

We use Ivy's notes because they're actually legible, and we follow each step to the letter. After the paper has turned to ash and we turn on the lights, I ask Ivy, "Do you think the spell actually makes you focus more? Or do you think you focus more because you cast a spell? And you trick your brain into thinking the spell makes you smart. Like the placebo effect. Remember that? We learned about that in science last year."

Ivy looks at me like I've gone a little crazy. "Huh?"

I shake my head. "Never mind." Is the spell making me too analytical? Because I've got plenty of that in me. I definitely don't need any more.

After thirty minutes of studying, I have to admit I feel more focused, but it's time to take a break.

I yawn, stretch my arms over my head. I look at Ivy sitting across from me on the floor. There's a light blue mist behind her that doesn't make any sense. I shut my eyes tight, rub them. I knew I was tired, but now I'm hallucinating. That can't be good.

When I open my eyes, the blue mist is still there. I point behind her. "Do you see that?"

She looks behind her and shakes her head. "What am I looking for?"

"You don't see anything?"

She turns back around. "Hmmm. Nope."

My throat tightens, and Ivy reaches over the candle and touches my arm. My fear fizzles through her, and she pulls her hand back. "Why are you so afraid?"

"I don't know," I want to say. Instead I tell her, "I'm just tired. Guess I'm seeing things."

She looks at me hard. "I'm not buying it."

I shrug it off. "I'm fine. I didn't sleep well last night. That's all."

She leans back against the bed. "You know you can tell me what's bothering you."

"It's nothing!" There's just a blue mist surrounding you that only I can see. What's wrong with that? I feel slightly—okay, a lot—hysterical.

"Okay," she says, "You keep forgetting I'm an empath. You can't hide your feelings from me. I'll get the story out of you. You know it's just a matter of time."

"Yeah, yeah." I finally force a swallow, and it feels like I've shoved a tennis ball down my throat. She's right, of course. She'll figure it out. But for now the blue mist is my secret. I want to make sure I'm not going crazy first.

I put my notebook back on my lap and begin working on another fraction problem, but I can't focus and Ivy's in the mood to talk.

"Did you ever ask Cody about the rumor Jo and Dru heard?"

I put my notebook down. "You mean the completely ridiculous rumor that he's some kind of royalty at Riley? Uh, no. Because, you know, I'd sound like an idiot."

Ivy shakes her head. "There's something to this, Hal. I'm telling you. I *feel* it."

"Quit playing the empath card," I tell her. "You're wrong about this."

"Why can't you at least ask him about it?"

I picture Cody and his hair hanging over his eyebrows. And his smile, which would surely turn to hysterical laughing if I asked him such a thing.

"I'm not going to leave you alone until you ask him," Ivy says.

"Good luck."

The blue mist is still there, and I'm beginning to think it's not because I'm tired. But I'm way too scared to say anything about it. This is a question for Lady Rose or Miss A, whomever I see first. I look at the clock. Five forty-five. Maybe I can get one of them alone at dinner. The hard part will be talking without the headmistress butting in or—worse—hearing my thoughts.

There's no way I can focus on math anymore, spell or no spell. The blue mist is all I can see.

I go to the bathroom, wash my hands, and splash cold water on my face. I use a towel to dry off, then pause before raising my head to look in the mirror. Do I really want to know if that same mist is behind me too?

Stop being so afraid. You have the most powerful gift in the building. Stand up on three.

One.

Two.

Three.

I stand straight up, keep my eyes closed. One deep breath and then I'll open them.

In.

Out.

No mist.

Relief runs through me. It had to be the lighting. The candle, the sunset. It had to be that. I'm going to walk back into our bedroom, and the mist will be long gone.

When I walk out of the bathroom, my hope vanishes. Ivy's sitting on her bed, pulling her hair back into a ponytail. And shining out around her entire body is the same light blue I saw before.

"What?" Ivy asks. "Don't knock my hair. I'm doing it without a mirror."

I have to get out of this room. Maybe seeing Ivy somewhere else will fix it. "Ready to go?"

My heart is beating so fast, I can feel it through my entire body.

Ivy looks at the clock. "We still have ten minutes. Want to keep studying till then?"

I almost laugh out loud. Concentrate on math when my best friend is swimming in a sea of colored mist and doesn't even know it? I don't think so.

"Nah, I think I'm done for now. Can I blow out the candle?"

Ivy shrugs. "Sure. I'm pretty hungry."

I put the spell ingredients onto my desk. I'm sure these are things we will use a lot. And maybe next time I'll be sane.

"Think it worked?" Ivy asks.

"What?"

"The spell, dummy. Think you were more focused?"

I was totally focused until you turned the air blue. "Umm, yeah, I guess so. You?"

"I definitely noticed a difference."

I follow Ivy out the door and into the empty hallway. The blue mist still hangs around Ivy. What is it?

By the time we reach the hall outside the dining room, I'm at least able to breathe normally, even if my hands are still shaking. We walk into the dining room, and whatever sense of peace I had two seconds ago abandons me.

I look at the head table, where the headmistress sits with the dorm mothers. The instructors have their own table, and I look there, too.

My eyes dart from table to table.

No, no, no, no, no.

I shut my eyes as hard as I possibly can, then slowly open them again. Slowly, slowly, slowly . . . My eyes are half open when I see it again.

The same mist thing that I saw on Ivy surrounds every single person in the room. But there are all kinds of different colors. Every possible shade of every possible color. It's like a rainbow threw up in the dining room.

I can hear Ivy saying something, but she sounds a thousand miles away.

Then someone wraps an arm around my shoulder and walks me out of the room.

Fourteen

I stumble beside Lady Rose, her voice soft and calming. "Ssh. It's okay. Hang on. Almost there."

She takes me into her classroom, closes the door, and sits me in her chair.

"Breathe with me. In two-three-four, out two-three-four."

I follow her breathing, and in a few minutes I don't feel like I'm going to die. Lady Rose squats in front of me, her hands on my knees and an orangey-red haze all around her.

"What do you see when you look at me?" she asks.

"Orange. Or red. Maybe a mix of the two."

She smiles and stands up. "That's wonderful. Perfect, actually."

I shake my head at her. "It feels the exact opposite of perfect."

She drags a chair over and sits in front of me. "Let me explain what's happening, Hallie."

"Please. In case you haven't noticed, I'm losing it. I'm going crazy here."

She pats her soft hand on my sweaty one. "You are not going crazy. You have inherited another gift."

My mind rewinds in warp speed. "But I've been so careful. I haven't touched anything that wasn't mine."

"Yes, you have," she says. "You borrowed my pen today. Remember?"

In that moment everything becomes clear. The pen. The colors.

"I inherited your gift."

"You did. Well, if you want to get technical, you inherited my mother's gift. It was her pen you were using. She gave it to me a few years before she died. I didn't think about it until after I'd put the pen in your hand. That's interesting," she says, teacher turned scientist observing her test subject.

"How?"

"My mother was a medium. Can you hear or see spirits?" she asks.

I shake my head. "No." I hope I never do.

"So you inherited *my* gift, not my deceased mother's. That's different than what we thought."

I don't like the way this sounds. Like everyone is watching me to see what freakish thing happens next. Like I'm an alien that must be dissected and figured out.

"Honestly, Hallie, I think you'll find this gift helpful. And I can help you read them."

"Read what?"

"Those colors you're seeing behind everyone? Those are their auras."

"How is that going to help me?"

She folds her arms over her chest. "For starters you can figure out right away what people are like. No more surprises when someone spreads a rumor about you. You will know not to trust someone if their aura is deep purple."

I don't say anything. "I didn't even know auras were real. I thought it was one of those hippy things."

Lady Rose laughs. "No, Hallie, they're very real. Let me ask you something. What color is Ivy's aura?"

"Blue. Light blue."

Lady Rose nods. "Yup. She's all the things that light blue represents. Peaceful, honest, intuitive."

"So you can see all these colors too?" I ask her.

She nods. "For almost twenty years now."

"Do they go away? Or will I always see them?"

"Once you've seen them, you'll always see them."

"I can't live like that. It's too distracting."

"I felt that way at first too. Trust me. You get used to it."

I find that incredibly hard to believe.

"Yeah, I know you find it hard to believe. We really need to work on your mind control. Every single thought you have comes into my head. It gets a little annoying."

She laughs, and I try to laugh with her, but it comes out sounding more like a psychotic sob.

"Why don't I have an aura?" I ask her.

"You do. We just can't see our own. Want to know what your color is?" she asks.

"I don't know. Do I?"

"You, my dear, are a brilliant shade of yellow."

I look around me but don't see anything.

"We can't see our own auras. But trust me, yours is impressive."

"What does yellow mean?" Confused? Intimidated? Overwhelmed?

"Yellow is a wonderful color. People with yellow auras

are full of inner joy, very generous, and not attached to material things. You've had that color since the first day we met over a year ago. I've never seen it change. Most girls your age change quite a bit."

My panic slowly subsides, and I let the questions come.

"How do you know what the colors mean?"

"I'll give you a list." She reaches into her desk and pulls out a small laminated card. Every color is listed, and beside it is its meaning.

"It's that simple?" I ask.

"Yep. It's really that simple."

"Can our auras change?"

"Absolutely. As people change, so do their auras. Now, I'm not talking about physical changes. I'm talking about fundamental beliefs, motivations, that kind of thing. Only then will an aura change."

I let it all sink in, and I lean back in the chair. I want to ask her about the dream. But I don't think I can handle any more tonight.

"Ready to eat something?" she asks.

"I just want to sleep."

"Go to your room. I'll have Miss A bring you a sandwich, and I'll tell Ivy you're okay."

"She won't believe you."

Lady Rose laughs. "You're probably right. But I can be pretty convincing."

I nod, grateful I don't have to face anyone right now.

I walk in silence with Lady Rose. When we get to the dining room, she stops, puts her hand on the door handle, and turns around. "Go get some rest, okay?"

"Thank you," I tell her. I'm just a few steps away when she says my name again.

"Hallie? We can talk about the dream anytime you're ready."

Ivy, with her aura, gets to the room twenty minutes after I do.

"You scared the bejesus out of me. Don't do that again, please. You're the unshakeable one, remember?"

I don't feel unshakeable. Not today.

Miss A bursts into the room. She couldn't do discreet if she had to. Especially not with the neon green aura around her. It clashes with her orange hair but somehow looks just right on her. "Well, aren't you just the most pitiful little thing I've ever laid eyes on."

There's something about Miss A that just makes me

feel better. Safer. Like I'm not in this alone. I want to pull the list of auras from under my pillow and see what her color means. Maybe she's green because she's a hedge witch. That's what I thought I would be, since that was what my great-great-grandmother Elsa was, but no such luck. Everyone says they'd kill for my gift of inheritance. But it's hard to control, and quite frankly, it's exhausting.

Miss A puts a plate of food on my desk. "Cheese and cucumber sandwich. Your favorite."

"Thanks, Miss A."

"Glory be, sugar. You have to slow down a little and get some rest. I bet you didn't sleep more than a few hours last night, did you? I mean, look at those gray bags under your eyes. Maybe you should take those cucumbers off the sandwich and put them on your eyes. They say that's good for swollen eyes. I've never tried it, mind you. But some people just swear by it."

Miss A's rambling has me giggling, and I reach over and hug her. "Have I told you how much I love you?"

"Well, now, the feeling's mutual, darling. Let's get you some rest tonight, and everything will feel better in the morning."

I give her a little salute. "Yes, ma'am."

Miss A looks at Ivy. "I'm counting on you to make sure she takes it easy tonight. No late-night studying or gossiping. That can wait for another day."

We both nod, and we all know we're lying.

Miss A leaves, and Ivy turns to me. "We were talking at dinner, and we've decided you have to e-mail Cody."

I look into Ivy's excited eyes. "Uh-uh. Not going to happen."

"Just hear me out," she says, holding her hand over my mouth to keep me from talking.

"You've got ten seconds," I say through her fingers.

She pulls her hand away. "Kendall and Zena are scheming to do something at the Third Harvest celebration. And it involves Cody. Jo's been listening to their conversations all week."

"What do you mean, it involves Cody?" I sit up in bed, take the sandwich from my table. I pull the cucumbers off and eat them first.

"Jo says they're talking about 'getting him.' We don't know if that means, like, boyfriend-and-girlfriend stuff. Or if it means they want to take him down."

"And how is me e-mailing Cody going to help?"

"Oh my gosh. You really are tired. You e-mail Cody,

find out if he's really some kind of royalty. If he is, you warn him that Kendall and Zena are targeting him for something. If he isn't, then we . . . Well, I guess we still have to warn him, don't we?"

I pop another cucumber into my mouth. "We do. So there's really no reason for me to e-mail him about the ridiculous rumor."

Ivy turns whiny. "Please, Hallie. We just want to know. You know you want to know too. Stop pretending that you don't."

"If I e-mail him, will you please drop it?"

She nods, but she knows and I know that she will never drop it. Especially if it turns out to be true. Which it won't.

I can do one of two things here. I can either stand my ground and deal with the nonstop pleading and harassment from Ivy or I can send the stupid e-mail and live in peace.

"Fine," I say. I hand her my plate and pull the laptop from my desk.

Fifteen

I log in and see two e-mails from Cody.

"He's been e-mailing you, Hallie!" Ivy's voice is a near-shriek. I put my hands over my ears and close my eyes.

"Please, Ivy," I say. "My head is already pounding."

"Sorry, sorry," she says, back to a whisper. "What do they say?"

This is the kind of thing I really wanted to avoid. It's why I didn't want to tell anyone about us e-mailing, because I knew it'd turn into this. A three-ring circus centered on my love life. And it's not love, so I can't even call it that.

"Tell me," Ivy says. "I'm your best friend. You're supposed to tell me things like this. It's practically a rule."

"You wear me out sometimes," I tell her.

I click on the first e-mail from Cody and read it out loud.

"We spent all day in the woods behind our campus, practicing some 'outdoor' gifts. This one guy named Jason has the gift of aerokinesis. He can control the wind, and it's wicked cool. Maybe he can show you at the celebration."

"Hey," Ivy says. "Maybe Jason's cute. Maybe we can be a couple. Maybe we can double-date."

"Maybe you can relax," I reply.

"Open the next one," she prods.

I open the e-mail and begin reading. *"You know how I told you I had the gift of invincibility—"*

"Wait," Ivy interrupts. "What the heck is that?"

"It means you can't be beat."

Ivy's nose scrunches up. "He's always the winner?"

"Always."

"Will he live forever?" she asks.

I give her a sharp look. "Of course not." At least I don't think so. "It's the highest gift you can have at Riley."

"And you have the highest possible gift at Dowling. See?" she says. "You're perfect for each other. Keep reading."

I go back to the e-mail. *"Well, it turns out I am also a*

scryer. If you don't know what that is, it means I can help find and locate missing or lost people."

"That is cool," I say to myself. Of course Ivy hears it.

"Ha! Admit it. You do like him."

"I like him. I never said I didn't like him."

"But you *like* like him."

I ignore her and continue reading the e-mail. *"What's kind of cool about that is, I can work with cops or whatever when a kid goes missing. Hope I never have to use it on someone I know. Gotta run. See you at the celebration."*

"What's the P.S.?" Ivy asks.

"P.S. Is it a kissing booth?"

"Ooooh!" Ivy jumps up and down like she's on an invisible trampoline. "He wants to kiss you."

I hold up a hand to stop her burgeoning overreaction.

"Calm down already. Did you ever think I might not *want* to kiss him?"

She crosses her arms over her chest. "Fine. But we both know I'm right. And we both know you want to kiss him."

I try to shove from my brain the image of Cody kissing me, but now that it's there, I can't get rid of it.

"What exactly do you want to know from Cody?" I ask. "Let's write this e-mail and get it over with."

I click the compose button and then type in Cody's e-mail address.

"You have to ask him if he's going to be the High Priest of the Riley coven one day."

I shake my head, eyes closed. "I can't believe I'm doing this."

```
To: codyray@rileyacademy.edu
From: halliecat@dowling.edu
Re: Stupid Question (sorry)
Hi, Cody. I would love to see Jason
control the wind. That sounds cool. But
none of that compares to being a scryer. I
think that's awesome.
```

I want to tell him about the auras, but I can't. Not with Ivy reading over my shoulder. I look back at the e-mail.

```
So, some friends of mine heard a rumor,
and they are begging me to ask you about
it. I finally gave in. I know this is
going to sound superstupid, and I don't
know why I agreed to e-mail you about it,
```

but here it goes. The story is that you
are part of some sort of Riley royalty and
one day you'll be Riley's High Priest. I
know, I know, I know. Stupid. Just send
back the no, and I'll get them off my back.

    See you soon,

    Hallie

I click send and close my laptop. "There. Happy?"

Ivy gives me a hug and a big smile. "I am. Thank you!"

"Why is this so important to you?"

"Hallie, don't you—just once—want to know more than Zena and Kendall? Seriously, how sweet does that sound? And if the rumor's true and he likes you instead of one of them, *and* he's crazy powerful? Even better."

"I've got to admit, that sounds pretty darn good."

"You have to start listening to me," Ivy says. "I'm always right about these things."

It takes me two hours to fall asleep. And when I do, my dream about Cody reveals more details. But it still doesn't make any sense.

A ding from my phone wakes me, and I think it's my

alarm. But the clock says it's only two forty-four. I lie back in bed, grab my journal, and write the new details, using my phone for light.

Destiny.
Repeated over and over and over like an endless echo.
Cody.
Kendall.

So, does this mean that Kendall and Cody are "destined" to be together? There's no way that's right. Cody doesn't like her. He told me so himself.

If I could see my aura right now, I think it'd be dark green, because jealousy boils inside me.

I put the journal back on my desk and check my phone to see what the ding was for.

I have a new e-mail.

Good. Maybe Cody has replied and I can shut my friends up once and for all.

I click the e-mail icon, and sure enough, Cody's reply is in my inbox. I click it open, and everything in my world comes to a screeching stop.

```
To: halliecat@dowling.edu
From: codyray@rileyacademy.edu
Re: Stupid Question (sorry)
We need to talk about this face-to-face,
Hallie. I'll tell you everything at the
celebration.
```

I reread the message. I freeze.

I turn off my phone and put it on the desk. Click the lamp on.

Ivy doesn't move. But I need her to wake up. I've got to tell her. It can't wait.

"Ivy," I say, my voice just louder than a whisper. She rolls over in bed, and I say her name again.

"Ivy."

Her eyes squint open. "What's wrong? Can't sleep again?"

"Cody e-mailed me back."

She shoves her body into a half-sitting position. "What? What'd he say?"

"That he'd talk to me about it in person at the celebration."

Ivy's jaw drops. "No. Way."

I nod, panic building. "What does it mean if he's going to be?"

"I think it just means he'll be the leader of the coven. He'll probably get to choose what he wants to do when he's done with school."

I look at the dream journal on my desk. I've got to tell her about it.

"So, my dream journal," I say. "I've been dreaming about what's going to happen with Cody."

"And?" she asks, leaning off the side of her bed like a lion ready to pounce.

I tell her about the dreams, everything I can remember.

"I think I know what's going on," Ivy says. "Just think about it. You're constantly fighting Kendall for what you want, right?"

"Yeah," I say.

Ivy sits back again, nodding her head. "This is just more of the same. You're worried Kendall will somehow magically snap Cody right out of your grasp. But that will never happen."

"If only you were psychic," I say. "Anyway, all of this is way too deep. We're only twelve. What do I care if some middle school boy doesn't like me?"

"Hallie . . ."

"I have too many other things to worry about than some boy. That's that."

I don't say that I'm really afraid of what it would mean if I was dating the High Priest. Would I have to follow certain rules? Call him Your Majesty?

I flop over in bed, ending the conversation.

But the word "destiny" echoes endlessly in my head. At Dowling we believe in destiny. If Kendall and Cody are destined to be together, how in the world can I change it?

Because I *have* to change it. Cody deserves so much better than the meanest good witch at Dowling.

Sixteen

The next couple of days fade into one another. I ignore Cody's e-mails because I don't know what to say. And it doesn't even matter. After all, he's just a boy. If the headmistress put her head to it, she could figure out a way to get me excommunicated. I'm not risking my gifts on some guy I hardly know.

Lady Rose was right. The auras do become normal. I play a game with myself where I guess what someone's aura will be before I see them. Kendall and Zena are usually surrounded by a gray aura, which is the sign of dark thoughts. No big surprise. That was hardly a challenge.

Before my class with Lady Jennica, I guess she'll be turquoise, which means she's dynamic. A natural leader. And when I walk into class that day, I smile to myself when I see that blue-green aura behind her. I'm pretty good at this game. I wish I could play it with Ivy. For some reason my gut tells me to keep this a secret. Maybe I'm just being paranoid.

Lady Jennica's room has a lab behind our desks. Today those lab tables hold stacks and stacks of old books. The scent of aged paper fills the room. I love the smell of books. Old, new, it doesn't matter. I start walking to the tables to see what the books are, when Lady Jennica calls my name.

"Can you come here for a minute?"

My hands instantly turn sweaty. Am I in trouble? I'm not used to being in trouble. I will do almost anything to keep out of trouble.

"Relax," she says when I get to her desk. "You're not in trouble."

I give her a nervous nod.

Her voice lowers, and I have to strain to hear her. "How are you doing?"

I know she is asking about something specific, but I don't know what it is. "Okay."

Lady Jennica gives me the same look Lady Rose gave me. The one that says she wants to tell me more than she's allowed to. "Good. Good." Her voice is strained, like she doesn't believe my answer.

We stand in awkward silence for a full minute before I ask if I can go to my desk. She doesn't answer immediately. She looks at me, her eyes so serious it makes me dread what's coming next.

"Hallie," she says. "I am forbidden to say anything specific."

"But . . ."

"Do me a favor?"

"Sure."

"Be more careful than normal."

I nod, confusion and fear making it impossible to speak.

"Promise me," she says.

"I promise."

She sighs deeply and gives me a half smile, and I walk back to my desk.

"Everyone, sit down," she says, snapping her fingers to close the door. Lady Jennica sits on her desk, her legs crossed in perfect form. Her face is back to normal, and she's in teacher mode.

"I know there's a lot of excitement in the air about the

upcoming Third Harvest celebration," she begins. The volume escalates quickly until she holds up her hand, her *Zip it* sign. "As I was saying, I know you're fired up, but you really need to focus today. We are digging into the genealogy. You should already have completed your basic family tree with your parents, grandparents, and great-grandparents. Let's get those papers out. Then I'll have you add a sheet to the bottom so you can continue the search."

Lady Jennica passes out the extra paper, and we all tape it to the bottom of our family trees.

"Now, girls, I'm going to warn you. This search can be time consuming and tedious. But it's critical you know who came before you. You must be careful that you copy the information down *exactly* as it is written. Do not rush."

She dives into a fifteen-minute lecture about always wearing these thin white gloves when looking in the books because the oil from our hands can cause the paper to deteriorate. She then tells us how the books are organized. By the time she allows us to begin our research, my head is swimming.

I know I have to look up my great-great-grandmother in the S book for "Simon." I have to wait for two people in front of me to finish looking before I can get to the book. And when I do, I'm speechless. The pages are yellow and thin, the handwriting meticulous. I'm awed by the fact that I'm looking at writing put on paper a hundred or more years ago. I think about my descendants and what they'll think of me when they find my name in one of these books.

I carefully turn the pages until I find Elsa's name in the register. I copy down the information on my paper.

Elsa Whittier Simon
Born: 06 July 1902
Dowling Ancestor: Bridget May Whittier
Entered Dowling: 01 September 1922
Graduated Dowling: 06 June 1929
Gift: Hedge Witch

I keep my paper steady and write as neatly as possible. If I write it neatly this time, I won't have to do it over.

I've always been a history buff, but knowing that this history is directly related to me fuels my curiosity even more than normal. Lady Jennica walks through the room to make sure everyone is working.

When she gets to me, she looks over my shoulder. "So now you need to find Bridget's name in the *W* book."

"Yes, ma'am."

I stack my papers neatly, grab my pen. When I turn around, I run right into Kendall. The same depressing gray haze surrounds her, like she's walking around in a storm cloud.

"I'm surprised you don't have this done already. You've always been such a little overachiever."

As much as I hate talking to Kendall, seeing her up close and watching her forked tongue appear and disappear, appear and disappear, is so gratifying that I forget I don't want to talk to her.

"Yeah, well, I've been busy. Cody e-mails me constantly." Before a word can slither out of her, I point at Kendall's mouth. "Good luck with all that."

I turn around and focus on the book, hands shaking. Why did I say that about Cody? I'm just making a bad situation worse. I never should have said that. But I so rarely get to put Kendall in her place, it just flew right out. I grin to myself. I can't wait to tell Ivy, Jo, and Dru. They'll be so proud of me.

I open the *W* book and begin looking for Bridget's

name. I wish the registers had photographs or drawings of our ancestors. I finally find her, the last name on page 422 of the book.

> Bridget May Whittier
> Born: 20 March 1890
> Dowling Ancestor: Anna Cooper Hewitt
> Entered Dowling: 29 August 1900
> Graduated Dowling: 11 May 1908
> Gift: Telekinesis

"Thirty more minutes, girls," Lady Jennica calls out. I look for Ivy, but find Kendall glaring at me. I ignore her and walk to Ivy's table.

"Isn't this cool?" I ask. Ivy's paper has only one name added. "What's taking you so long?"

She gives me an irritated look. "I got stuck waiting behind Zena. She took her sweet time finding the name she was looking for. Even stopped to redo her ponytail like I wasn't even standing there. She finally left when Lady Jennica told her to move on."

I take a quick glance at Zena, whose aura has become darker than Kendall's. No surprise there.

"Wait for me after class," I tell Ivy. "I have to tell you about my conversation with Kendall."

Her eyes widen. "Oh boy, can't wait to hear that."

I walk on to the *H* book. Missy is working in it, so I wait behind her. I guessed her aura right too. She's pink—the perfect balance between spirituality and materialism. "Going okay?" I ask her.

She nods, face content, like always. I wish I could be like that. She always seems to feel exactly the same. She finishes her work, then gives me a little wave when she walks away.

I find Anna's name and begin writing.

Anna Cooper Hewitt
Born: 13 August 1869
Dowling Ancestor: Sarah Elizabeth Scott
Entered Dowling: 08 September 1880
Graduated Dowling: 31 May 1888
Gift: Blinking

I stop and look at that again. Blinking is a gift? I wave to Lady Jennica, and she walks over. She looks at my paper, and her eyes squint, like maybe she can't read something that far away or she's waiting for me to say something. I know for a fact the handwriting is neat.

"What kind of gift is blinking?"

Lady Jennica smiles. "It's not what you think."

"Good, because it sounds super-lame."

She laughs and then explains. "Blinking is instant teleportation, activated by thinking of a location and blinking your eyes."

I stare at her, openmouthed. "Shut. Up." I slap a hand over my mouth. "I'm so sorry, Lady Jennica! I didn't mean—"

She shakes her head at me. "It's fine, Hallie."

"How cool would that be?" I wonder out loud.

"Well, Hallie, you know you can have any gift you want. All you have to do is find the right item from your ancestor."

I shake my head. "I've got my hands full with the three gifts I've picked up accidentally."

"I don't know about that, Hallie. Your family line has some pretty amazing gifts." She gives me a wink, then leaves to help another student.

I look at my paper again to make sure I've copied down everything correctly. As I reread the gifts of my ancestors, my skin begins to tingle. Maybe Lady Jennica's right. Maybe acquiring some of these gifts might not be so bad after all.

Seventeen

Lady Rose reminds everyone to review their dream journals daily and to record in them when they wake up. I have been keeping my journal, but nothing has changed in my dreams. I *always* have the Cody and Kendall dream.

"How has the studying spell been going for everyone?" Lady Rose asks.

Ivy raises her hand. "I got my first A on a math test after we did the studying spell in our room."

"Super," the teacher says. "Anyone else?"

Several students answer, but I don't hear them. My eyes, energy, every cell are obsessing over Kendall. Lady Rose claps her hands and jolts me back to class.

"Today we're going to learn a protection spell. There

are all kinds of protection spells, but we're starting small. This one will keep you safe from illness, and it will give you the necessary wisdom to keep you safe."

Fitting. The headmistress wouldn't think twice about making me disappear. She will stop at nothing to make sure Zena is at the top of the Dowling food chain.

"There are some important things to remember about this spell. The first thing you need to know is that it doesn't make you invincible. You can't cast this spell, then go rob a bank and expect nothing to happen to you."

Everyone in the room laughs, but I think about Cody and how his gift of invincibility probably means he doesn't ever have to do this spell.

"Second. You should save this spell for a time when you're feeling particularly vulnerable. Magic isn't intended to protect you from every single thing that might happen. This is for the biggies."

I make those notes in the margin, then write "Protection Spell" in my favorite fancy letters. When they find my dead body clutching my Book of Shadows after I've been eliminated as the next High Priestess, at least they'll be impressed with my supercute lettering, right?

"Okay," she says with a quick *clap, clap* of her hands.

"Let's get started. You should notice that the only ingredient for this spell is a white candle. I prefer casting this spell outside, but you can do this wherever you happen to be."

She picks up the candle, lights the wick with her fingers, and looks back up. When she does, she's looking right at me in a superintense and intimidating way, like she's trying to tell me something with her eyes. When she speaks, her voice is low and soft, and each word is enunciated with deliberate care.

"You must stand facing west. Then you'll recite the chant."

"Protect me with all your might,
oh, Goddess Gracious, day and night."

I'm writing quickly, and it's not as neat as I'd like, but I don't want to miss anything. When I finally take my eyes off the paper to see what she does next, she's staring at me again. No one else in the room seems to notice, but I do, and it's totally creepy.

"You will then turn to the north and repeat the chant."

She turns and chants.

"Then the east."

She turns and chants.

"Then the south."

She turns and chants.

"Then back to the west to end with 'So mote it be.'"

By the time the bell rings, I'm exhausted from trying to learn all of this new knowledge.

Ivy and I are walking out when Lady Rose calls me back in. "It'll just take a minute, Hallie."

I look at Ivy, and she shrugs before walking off. Getting kept after class is becoming a thing with me, and I don't like it. I just want to be normal. Whatever that means at Dowling.

Lady Rose waits for the room to empty before speaking to me. "Lady Jennica says she spoke to you. That she told you to be careful."

I nod. "Yes, ma'am. She did. So your protection spell today was great timing."

Lady Rose gives me a knowing grin. "That wasn't a coincidence."

I take a deep, deep breath. "What exactly is going on?"

Lady Rose looks at me so long, I wonder if she's been frozen by someone's spell. I look at my watch and then wave my hands in front of her face. "Uh, Lady Rose? Are you okay?"

She blinks, disoriented, like a baby waking from a nap. "I'm so sorry. Mind must have wandered off."

"Can you tell me what I need to be protecting myself from?" I ask. "Because all these warnings aren't going to do me a lot of good if I don't know what to watch for."

She shakes her head, of course. "You know I can't. But I do have something for you."

Lady Rose turns around and grabs her sleek black leather purse. She reaches inside a hidden pocket and pulls out a barrette. But it's no ordinary barrette. This one is covered in dark red stones and tiny little clear crystals. "That's beautiful," I tell her.

"I'd like you to have it," she says.

I shake my head. "I can't."

"Of course you can. My grandmother gave this to me years ago, before she died. Now when I wear it, I feel like she's watching over me. I feel safer. I think you could use some of that, don't you think?"

I do. Of course I do. But . . .

"I'll inherit her gift."

"No, Hallie. She wasn't a witch."

"Are you sure?"

She gives me a look. "Of course I'm sure."

So I nod. "I'll take wonderful care of it. I promise I won't break it."

Lady Rose smiles. "I'm not worried about that. Not worried about that at all."

Eighteen

Every time I look in the mirror, I have to stare a few extra seconds. I love my ocean-blue eyes.

If I didn't detest Kendall so much, I'd thank her for them. Who knows what kind of spell she was attempting. Probably to make me blind. I don't know why she even bothers when she knows her spells will reflect her white magic. No matter how hard she tries, she can't cast a black magic spell. It's ironic, actually. If we could swap gifts, we'd both be happier. But maybe that's why we didn't get those gifts. Maybe this is supposed to help us somehow.

Today's the day we present our genealogy reports, and I haven't slept a wink all night. My dad and I once watched this documentary that traced the evolution of humans. After we watched it, Dad claimed everyone was related to everyone else in some way.

Maybe he's right. Maybe all of our paths cross at some point, like some giant maze we can't get out of.

I run a hand over my hair to tame the fly-aways, and take a huge, trembling breath.

It's just a regular day, I tell myself.

Somewhere, deep inside the recesses of my memory, I hear Kendall mocking me.

Nothing has ever bothered Kendall. Even when we were still friends, she was so confident. She never worried about her grades, friends, making her parents happy, or getting in trouble. That kind of personality always attracts a lot of people.

Kendall insists on having a take-no-prisoners mentality. She's first, and everyone else is second. It's kind of funny that she can't see that everything she does goes against the person—or witch—she was created to be. White magic witches bring peace, comfort, and prosperity to others. That's Kendall's purpose, but she doesn't realize it. Or maybe she does and doesn't accept it.

So.

If Kendall's fighting her white magic destiny by attempting black magic spells, what does that say about me?

Am I doing exactly the same thing by refusing the power of my own black magic destiny?

Lady Jennica's room is buzzing. Everyone's family tree has been carefully rolled and tied with a string. We are planning to unveil them today, share them with the class, then hang them outside our bedroom doors. I've worked so hard and so long on this project, I've memorized every detail written on it.

One by one we begin sharing. Turns out family tree presentations are one big snooze-fest. About halfway through the third girl, I'm fighting to stay awake. We're picked randomly so I have to stay alert. Otherwise I might pull a little disappearing act with my inherited gift of invisibility and take a nap.

Ivy goes before me, as do Jo and Dru. The most exciting thing about any of theirs is that Ivy is related to the second High Priestess of Dowling, Griselda Blackwood. That's cool, and I'm a tiny bit jealous.

Finally, just as I'm about to pass out from boredom, Kendall is called. She walks to the front of the room, holding her family tree casually. Like she couldn't care less about her family heritage. You'd think if you spent this much time on a project, you'd at least pretend to be ready to present. But that's Kendall for you.

She unties the string, and her family tree unravels. Then she begins reading the names.

The witches in her family tree, like mine, like everyone's, have different gifts. Some are inherited, but it seems like most of the gifts are unique. Of course, no one in her family line has the gift of inheritance.

Kendall's voice is monotone, her speech interspersed with plenty of instances of "um's" and "like's." She reads from the paper with the enthusiasm of a man walking to his own execution. She adds nothing interesting about her ancestors. Just reads the information like she's reading a phone book.

And then.

Then.

Then I hear it.

"Sarah Elizabeth Scott."

That name. I know that name.

Breathe.

It's on my *own* family tree.

There's no way.

How can we have the same ancestor? My mind cramps, hands sweat.

We're related.

Ivy puts her hand on my back. "What's wrong?" she whispers. Her empathy must be off the charts, because my emotions are all over the place.

I sit up but can't face Ivy. If I see her eyes reflecting my own emotions, I'll lose it.

Kendall reads the rest of the details about Sarah. The details I've already memorized. They are, of course, exactly the same. I don't have to wonder if Kendall knows we share an ancestor. If she knew, she would have made some scene or refused the assignment, or something even worse, like burned the genealogy books. And she would. She is just that evil.

The rest of her presentation moves along at a snail's pace, and I have to fight to keep my feet from racing out of the room. Ivy doesn't say anything else, but I know she's watching me. Ready to hold me down if she has to.

Several more girls present their family trees. Then it's my turn.

My heart is pounding. I fumble as I try to untie the

string that is holding the scroll together, until Lady Jennica does it for me.

"You okay?" she whispers to me under her breath.

I don't answer, just unroll the family tree and face the class.

I had learned so much about my ancestors that I wanted to mention, things that aren't written on the paper, but that plan is toast. I'll be lucky to read the names without hyperventilating.

My voice squeaks out the first name, then the next, and the next. I don't relax. I can't.

I keep my eyes on Ivy, whose face is willing me to read the names and get back to my desk. There will be time enough for screaming and crying later.

And then it's time for me to say her name. I don't look at Kendall to see if she's watching me. I just take a breath and force the name out.

"Sarah Elizabeth Scott." I barely hear my own voice, and the hair on my arms stands up, as if the power in this room is supercharged.

"Wait a moment," Lady Jennica says, eyes squinted. "That name . . ."

"Was on mine," Kendall says, her voice icy. Furious. Like I *want* us to be related.

I close my eyes, wishing I were related to anyone at Dowling besides her. Even Zena would be better than Kendall. At least she didn't single-handedly ostracize me in elementary school.

Lady Jennica puts her hand on my back, holds her other hand up to quiet the now chaotic class. But I don't hear them talking, don't hear a single thing except the rapid-fire pulse in my ears, the sound of my life crumbling down around me.

"I told you these projects could be surprising," she says. She gives a nervous laugh. She's as surprised as I am. "Well, now, that *is* a surprise. How exciting. Right, class?"

The room is still, quiet. But the energy is so thick, I can barely breathe. I make myself look at Kendall. Her face is red, her eyes like fire.

"All right, then," Lady Jennica says. "Let's move on, shall we? Hallie, please continue."

I zip through the rest of my family tree. It's not like anyone is listening anyway. The two worst enemies at Dowling are related. No one really cares about anything else.

Soon enough I'm done with my presentation, and Lady Jennica rolls it up nicely for me. I guess she knows my hands are shaking too badly to do anything but wrinkle it.

"There now, Hallie," she says. "You be sure to hang that on your door when you get back to your room."

The thought of advertising that I am—in some infinitely distant and insignificant way—related to Kendall sends me reeling. I don't want to post it. I don't want to.

Lady Jennica pushes me back to my desk, and I sit down with a loud *whumph.*

"It's okay, Hal. Nothing's changed." Ivy gives me her best fake smile. "It's okay." She says the words, but neither of us believes them.

The class finishes the presentations. Not that I hear any of them after mine. I'm not sure anyone does. Lady Jennica finally dismisses us, and I can't get out of the room fast enough. But I see Kendall at Lady Jennica's desk and realize they're both looking at me.

I try to avoid them, get out of the room before either of them can grab me.

It's futile, of course. "Hallie," Lady Jennica says. Her voice is soft, almost apologetic.

The room clears out slowly, everyone wanting to hang back and hear what is said to the enemies-turned-relatives. Lady Jennica shoos them out and closes the door behind them.

She turns back toward us and manages a half smile. "Okay, girls. I know you are both upset about this."

Kendall lets out a loud scoff. "You think?"

I don't give her the satisfaction of reacting. Just keep my arms crossed and remind myself to breathe.

"This is rare. To have two witches connected at the fifth level who are so different."

"You can say that again." Kendall can't let a second go by without a jab.

"Different in terms of skill," Lady Jennica clarifies. I keep my eyes down. If I look at my teacher, I may start crying. "Typically those who are related have skills that are . . . better aligned. Black magic witches are related to other black magic witches, and vice versa. It makes me wonder . . ."

When she doesn't finish her sentence, I finally look at her. "Wonder what?"

She doesn't say anything, just looks at me, then Kendall, then back at me. She shakes her head slowly. "I don't know, to be honest."

"This has been extremely helpful," Kendall says under her breath.

I want out of this room, out of this building, out of this situation.

"Why don't you two go on to class? Let me get back to you on this, okay?" Lady Jennica asks the question but doesn't wait for our answer. She doesn't even say good-bye. She leaves the room, with us trailing close behind her.

Kendall shoves past me and walks toward our next class.

I stand in the hall and watch Lady Jennica. Her fast steps. Her shoulders set.

She's a woman on a mission to figure this out.

Nineteen

The Crafter Chamber has been converted into a mini art studio. Jo and Missy are walking the room, checking to see that we're drawing the tattoos correctly. Ivy and I volunteered to do the tattoos, along with the other dozen or so girls in here. The way I see it, if I'm busy with the tattoos, I don't have to deal with Kendall. And I have something to distract me if Cody falls into her trap.

"Kendall say anything to you?" Ivy asks. She keeps her voice low, knowing that others will eavesdrop. All week, whenever I passed people in the hallway, they stop their conversations. I've always wanted to be popular, for everyone to know who I am. But not like this. Like they're just waiting for me to self-destruct because I can't handle the pressure of being related to Kendall.

I shake my head at Ivy. "Are you kidding me?"

"I don't see what the big deal is. People in covens are related all the time. My sister and I would be in the same coven if she stayed committed to Dowling."

"But you both have white magic skills. She's a healer and you're an empath."

"And?"

I shrug, not entirely sure of the answer myself. "From what I've been able to read, which isn't a lot—there's absolutely nothing in the library about this—when two witches are related and one has white magic and the other has black magic, it's some sort of sign. The books don't say what kind of sign, just that certain things have to be done. Certain spells cast. None of that makes sense to me. I just want it to go away. I want to learn my spells, take my tests, and get through school with as little contact with Kendall as possible."

Ivy shakes her head. "I don't think that's in the cards."

Jo and Missy ring the chime sitting on Miss A's podium.

I'm surprised when Jo does the speaking. She's normally so shy, you don't even know she's in the room.

"Okay, everyone. It's nine, so we need to clean up and get back to our rooms. Thank you for helping. You're doing great."

We begin closing up our paints and putting paint-brushes into a cleaning liquid Jo's created. I blow on my posterboard and admire my work. When Miss A enters the room, she's a flurry of motion, her satin muumuu swirling around her like she's walking in a tornado.

"Hallie?" she calls, looking around the room. When she spots me, she beckons me toward her.

My back stiffens. Miss A has a wild look in her eyes, and that usually means something big has happened.

I follow her out of the room, and when we get to the hallway, she stops and looks both ways. When she decides it's safe, she grabs my hand and drags me behind her. She pulls me into her room, shuts the door, and locks it.

"You're starting to freak me out, Miss A."

She sits in her recliner and motions for me to sit on the coffee table in front of her. "Sorry, sugar. I just wanted to be the first to tell you. I sure didn't want you hearing it from someone else, especially one particular someone else. You know, in all my years, I've never seen anyone so full of hate. But that girl—"

I put my hand on hers to stop her rant. "What do you want to tell me?"

"I just came out of a meeting with Lady Jennica, Lady Rose, and the headmistress."

My gut screams *Prepare yourself.* "Lady Jennica has done quite a lot of research on this whole black magic versus white magic within families—"

"We are *not* family." I interject.

Miss A ignores my interruption and keeps talking. "I know you don't realize how rare this is. I've never encountered it in all the years I've lived here."

"What's the big deal? So what if we have different magic? Whoop-dee-freaking-doo!"

Miss A takes a deep breath, slows her pace. "Hallie, most covens choose to practice only one type of magic or the other. We are the only exception to that rule that I'm aware of. We are the only coven and the only school that not only allows both black and white magic but also teaches both."

"Okay," I say. "I still don't understand why this is important."

"The reason most covens operate that way is because combining the two types of magic is . . . well, it's difficult to maintain harmony in such environments."

"That makes sense, actually."

"Dowling has been able to do so successfully for centuries, and we pride ourselves on that accomplishment."

"And now?" I ask.

"And now we have a unique situation."

"And it involves me, of course."

She nods. "Indeed it does. Honey, there's something we've known but haven't shared with you. We wanted you to discover this on your own. We wanted to trust Saffra's timing. But it appears this is the time."

Secrets. More secrets. "Am I the only one who tells the truth around here?"

Miss A reaches forward and pulls me in for a quick hug. "I know it feels that way, but you can trust me, Hallie. Maybe more than you can trust anyone else in this building."

"So, what's the big secret? The big revelation?"

Even as I say the words, my chest tightens and every breath is a struggle.

"Hallie, sugar, you're destined to be the next High Priestess."

The air gets sucked out of the room and takes my heart with it.

"That's . . . that's impossible."

"Trust me. It isn't. It's in your bloodline, confirmed by your gift. To become the next High Priestess, there are many milestones you much reach and even more challenges to conquer."

I've always been an overachiever, but this is a little too much. Even for me. "What if I don't want to be High Priestess?"

Miss A flinches as if I've hit her. "It's not a matter of you wanting it, dear. You *will be* the High Priestess. Unless—"

"Yes! Let's explore that. Unless what?" I ask.

Miss A studies me, as if she's choosing what to tell me.

"No more secrets." My voice is firm, but still respectful, I hope.

"Well, this is where Kendall becomes part of the equation."

I close my eyes. Of course it's Kendall. I start laughing. "I can't escape her, can I?"

"Afraid not, Hallie. You see, she, too, has the ability to be the next High Priestess. Same bloodline and all. It would be harder for her to be the High Priestess without your gift, of course. I mean, most High Priestesses have the gift of inheritance. It's what makes them different from everyone else."

"But it can happen? A person can be the High Priestess without my gift?"

"She can. But it's much more difficult. With your gift, Hallie, you are practically unbeatable."

Practically.

"So, what does all this mean, Miss A?"

"Well, that's the interesting thing. That's why Lady Jennica's been so serious about this research. This hasn't happened. Not in recent history anyway. It turns out that when there are two potential High Priestesses, they must each prove their power over the other."

Me? Overpower Kendall?

"You can't be serious."

"Now, don't get all panicky on me. This wouldn't happen for years, of course. You two are both just learning how to be witches. It may be that one of you doesn't finish your training here at Dowling."

"Oh, I'm finishing," I tell her quickly.

"If one of you doesn't finish training," she says again, "the other would become High Priestess by default."

"By default? I don't want to win by default. I want to win fair and square."

What am I talking about? Am I really willing to go

toe-to-toe with Kendall? And what does that even mean? Do we have to fight? Or is there some Hunger Games–type competition we have to go through?

"Any win is a fair one." Miss A's voice is definitive, certain.

"I don't understand how we have the same bloodline. We have *one* relative in common."

"Yes, you're right. But it's not just any relative. Sarah Elizabeth Scott was the eldest daughter of Dowling's first High Priestess, Saffra Warnsly. Sarah's descendant is destined to be the next High Priestess. But she has two. You and Kendall. It would typically go to the eldest, but you are the same age."

I stand up. I have to move when I'm trying to figure something out. "So now what?" I ask.

"Now nothing. You continue to go through training, just as Kendall will."

"If she finds this out, she'll be even more determined than ever to ruin me."

"Which is exactly why I wanted to tell you what was going on. I suspect the headmistress will share the news with Kendall."

"Great," I say. "No doubt they're working on a plan to get me out of here."

"Even if they are," Miss A says, pulling me back down to the coffee table, "you are stronger than either one of them. Heck, honey, you're stronger than the two of them put together."

"Yeah, right."

"You have the power to inherit any gift you want or need. No one in this building, besides you, can do that. No one."

"What do I do, Miss A?" My eyes are swimming in tears.

"Sugar, you just keep on doing what you're doing. But you watch yourself with that Kendall Scott. You hear me?"

"I always do that."

She gives me a full-tooth smile. "Well, then, this won't change a thing, will it?"

Twenty

"You're trying to tell me *you* are going to be the next High Priestess?" Dru asks. She's the only one in the room who can speak.

The other two look through me, like they don't even see me.

I wave my arms back and forth in front of their faces. "Jo, Ivy."

Their eyes attempt to focus, and then all three of them break into a series of nonstop questions.

I hold up my hands to stop them. "I'm not done."

"There's more? How can there be more? I mean, you're going to be the . . . the High Priestess! Your picture will be in the hallway like Dannabelle's!" Ivy's out of breath by the time she finishes.

"It's not that easy," I tell her.

"Meaning?" asks Jo.

I launch into a regurgitation of what Miss A told me. With each new piece of information, they become more surprised, more alarmed, which only makes me feel more panicked.

Pull it together, Hallie.

Watching my friends, I realize I *have* to be a rock. I have to make them believe I'm not worried. Because I can't handle them freaked out.

"I need you to be my eyes and ears," I tell them. "I bet Kendall is being told tonight too. And if she thinks she has to beat me to get to the top, she'll come at me with everything she has."

They all agree, of course, and I trust them. I trust them more than I've ever trusted any other friends.

"When do you get to become High Priestess?" Dru asks.

"*If* I become High Priestess, it will be years after my training at Dowling, when I'm twenty-one."

"And until then you and Kendall are at war?" Ivy asks.

"Looks that way," I say. "It's not like Dowling can't survive without a High Priestess. The last one died four years ago."

"Well, I say you just keep doing what you're doing and try not to think about it. You know?" Jo is so sweet, I want to hug her. But she doesn't know my entire history with Kendall. Ignoring Kendall is a virtual impossibility. But I don't say so.

"You just make sure you keep your ears open, Jo," I tell her.

Ivy sticks her hand into the middle of our little circle. "We're all in this with you, Hallie."

Dru and Jo stack their hands on top of Ivy's. I'm afraid to talk, because talking might make me cry, and there's no crying in witchcraft, according to Miss A.

"All in," Dru says.

"All in," Jo echoes.

I put my hand on top of theirs and seal the pact. "All in."

If I thought I was going to live my life like normal, that no one would know what Miss A told me, I was wrong. So, so wrong.

When I enter the dining room for breakfast the following morning, the room is half full, as usual. The same girls are in there that we see every morning. But instead of girls yawning with their heads on the table or chatting with each other, everyone is staring at me. Some of them can't meet my eye but are whispering behind their hands. And I can tell that it is the oh-my-gosh-did-you-hear-about-Hallie kind of whispering. You'd think they'd be more interested in the celebration where they can hang out with boys than in me. And my power. And my future. I swallow the anxiety that is stuck in my throat, pull my shoulders back, and walk into the room as if I don't notice.

I quickly grab a plate, some fruit, and my favorite yogurt. I keep my face down and don't make eye contact with anyone until I get to our table.

"Good grief, is that what my life is going to be like?" I look at the girls at our table—my friends. They wear the same look that tells me they don't know what to say. If I thought I was living under a microscope before, I didn't know how bad it could be.

"It'll get better," Ivy says. "The new will wear off and things will go back to normal."

"Probably not, but thanks for trying," I tell her. "How did everyone find out?"

"Kendall and Zena, I'm sure."

I look at Ivy. "You're probably right. Knowing Kendall,

she's trying to get as many friends in her corner as possible."

Jo laughs. "Really? Who would believe a word she said? She's a liar, through and through. There's no changing that."

"I hear what you're saying, but I've known her my entire life. You'd be surprised how many will follow her."

"Well, that doesn't affect you at all," Dru says. "Remember your plan? Keep doing what you're doing. Learn. Be the best witch you can be. That's what will win this in the end."

"That's the thing. Do I even *want* to be High Priestess?"

Dru drops her fork onto the plate. The clang of silver on porcelain echoes off the walls. She looks at Ivy. "Is she for real?"

Jo shrugs. "I don't know, Dru. I think I see her point. It's a lot of pressure. And to get there, she has to fight Kendall for the next five years."

Ivy wipes her mouth, places her napkin on the table. She stacks her two plates, then the silverware on top. One big breath, then she looks at me. "Hallie, I'm your best friend. I will always love you. But if you bail out of this and leave us with Kendall as our leader, I will be forced to hate you. Why would you do that to us? To yourself? Are you really considering letting Kendall be the official boss of you? Forever?"

I look at my friends, all three of whom are now scared speechless at the prospect of having Kendall as the leader of the coven.

"Hallie, even if you don't want to do it for you, please do it for us. I'm begging you."

Dru leans closer, her big black eyes searching mine for a sign of hope. "Think about it. Do you want to be under Kendall's control again?"

I don't have to answer them. They know I'm going to fight it, because the only thing I hate more than Kendall is losing to Kendall.

The bell rings, and the cafeteria empties. I'm not quite finished eating yet, so I tell Ivy I'll catch up with her. I walk to the trash can slowly, popping the last of the grapes into my mouth. I dump my tray except for my yogurt and spoon. I can eat that on the way to class.

"Have a nice day, Hallie."

I smile at the cook behind the counter. It's the first time she's spoken to me, and I wonder why she'd start today. Is it possible even the cooks know?

My feet are in fast-forward when I turn around and slam right into Kendall. We both lose our balance and have to catch the wall to keep from falling.

"Of course it's you," Kendall says. "Who else?"

I know this is my chance to say something, but my mind is blank. It's always blank when I'm face-to-face with Kendall. And I'm supposed to be the High Priestess? Yeah, right.

Zena steps forward, pushing me out of the way with the backpack on her shoulder. "What are you doing here without all your little cronies?"

"Guess they've already figured out where the winning side is," Kendall says. Her laugh is mean, hateful, and entirely too familiar.

Zena grabs an apple from the buffet. "You know you're in way over your head, right?"

"According to who?"

Zena looks at Kendall like she doesn't understand what I'm saying. "Is she serious?"

Kendall rolls her eyes. "You have no idea how dense she can be."

"You can at least wait and talk about me after I leave," I tell Kendall. I step around her to get out and get to class. On my best day I break even with Kendall. And when it's two to one, I'm totally outnumbered.

I walk a couple of steps, grateful to put them behind me.

But. Wait. If I'm going to be the High Priestess, if I have any hope of being like Dannabelle, I have to start now. I have to be able to stand up for myself before I can take care of others.

I stand in the dining room, halfway between the buffet and the door to the hallway, at war with myself.

No one says I have to deal with Kendall today. I can save that for a day when I have some backup.

Or I can start right now. I can start being the person I was destined to be. A leader.

I toss the uneaten yogurt into the trash can and walk back to the buffet. Zena and Kendall are picking over the fruit and Danish left on the buffet. They're talking about me. Fury builds inside me as I listen to Kendall say all the things she's always said about me.

"She's useless. Everything she does is just . . . stupid. I'm telling you, this whole 'competition' is going to be a joke."

I step closer to the pair, and they turn around, surprised to see me but not embarrassed to be caught talking about me. That only fuels my anger more.

"Forget something?" Kendall asks, like she's happy to see me, like we aren't mortal enemies.

I stand strong, will my knees to stop shaking. And I give Kendall a smile.

"I did, actually. I forgot to tell you how much you bother me. For years I've kept quiet while you put me down. Shame on you for calling yourself a friend. And shame on you for hurting all the other girls you've ever met, just to fool yourself into believing you're better than everyone else." I take a giant step out of the buffet line and walk through the dining room. I'm going to be late for class, but I won't be as late as Kendall, who's still trying to figure out what just happened.

Twenty-One

I'd like to say that my little rant made a difference in the way Kendall acts, but it hasn't. If anything, it has made her treatment of my friends and me even worse. But something changed inside me when I stood up to her. I accepted that I want to be the High Priestess and I'm willing to fight for it.

I don't have time to deal with her right now, anyway. We've been busy preparing for the Third Harvest celebration. We have plenty of good painters to draw the tattoos onto people while everyone else takes turns working the booth. Turns out, I'm not too bad at painting tattoos. I don't have Jo's or Missy's creativity, but I can draw what they make up. After nonstop practice, mine look almost as good as Jo's.

Once our booth is made, we help other groups set up booths, decorate the grounds, line up chairs just right near the stage, and gather supplies. There's a charge of excitement at Dowling, and time slows to a crawl as we wait for the big day to arrive.

But the day finally comes. And it is a beautiful evening. Nice breeze. Full moon. I wonder if any of the witches at Dowling can control the weather.

We are allowed to wear regular clothes, so I'm in my favorite lace skirt and a red shirt. No glasses (thank you, Kendall). And Lady Rose's hair clip to add some bling.

When we walk out Dowling's front door, I feel like I'm in a different world. The grounds in front of Dowling have been transformed. Covered booths line the sidewalks. Benches and chairs are scattered in groups on the lawn. Picnic tables are set up near the garden, where food will be served. Candles are everywhere. Some are in holders that have been nailed into tree trunks, and some are at tables. Even more candles hang from the tree limbs. Custodians walk from candle to candle to light each one. Slowly the glow of candlelight warms the area for the celebration.

Jo has painted the design on my wrist, and I wish I could keep it there forever. It's the infinity sign made with a snake. It's said to symbolize that my gifts never end. They're always changing and growing as I learn.

I'm putting up the sign that shows all the tattoos we can do, when I hear the first rumble of buses driving through the Dowling gates.

I start to shake, and I have to tell myself to chill out. When the bus comes into view and we can see it's a Riley bus, Ivy is next to me, and she turns me to face her. She tries to smooth my hair down. "Enough," I tell her, pushing her hands away. "He'll see you."

I stand at the booth's entrance with the other girls and greet the boys as they get off the bus and begin walking around. I do my best to look for Cody without actually looking like I'm looking for him. Kendall and Zena haven't been seen all day, but I know they'll be here. They're just waiting to make their entrance.

A tall guy, whose nametag reads *Victor*, is our first customer. He has a misty gray aura. So he's materialistic and selfish. Maybe he should meet Kendall.

He asks me to paint the design of his gift on his upper arm. He explains that he is telekinetic, so I carefully paint the thin circles like a spring and a lightning bolt in the center.

"Can you show me how it works?" I ask him.

"What do you mean?" he asks. He's sitting so close to me, I can smell his breath, a mixture of breath spray and Fritos. Blech.

"I mean, can you do it? Like . . ." I look around and point to the candle sitting on the counter of our booth. "Move that candle?"

Victor looks around, nervous. "I don't know."

"Never mind," I say. "It's okay. I didn't realize you hadn't really mastered it yet."

He pulls back from me, eyes dark and challenging. "That has nothing to do with it."

He looks at the candle, and it slides to the other side of the counter.

The girls who see it clap, and one of them saves the glass candle holder from shattering against the side of the booth.

"Not too bad," I say. I go back to work on his design.

Until I hear Cody's voice.

"Vic, did I just see you move that candle?"

Vic looks up and I look up, and there he is.

My stomach is like a balloon just waiting to be popped. Tight. Tense.

He's cuter than I remember. His hair's longer, he's tanner, and he's taller. In dark blue jeans, boots, and a plain black T-shirt, he's just a little bit breathtaking. And surrounding all of that is a bright orange aura. He's a natural leader. The color fits him.

"I don't think so," he says. Vic looks at me. "Did I move that candle?"

I look around and shake my head. "What candle?"

"Cute," Cody says. "You know the rule. No magic. No showing off."

Cody hangs around the booth while I finish Vic's arm. Once Vic is gone, Cody walks to my chair. "Can I go next?" he asks.

"Be my guest," I tell him.

He sits down and looks at me closely. "Your eyes are different. Do you have on colored contacts?"

I shake my head. "Kendall messed up another spell, so now I have blue eyes and I don't need glasses."

He laughs. "A bad day to be Kendall."

I think about my run-in with Kendall in the cafeteria. I want to tell him about it, but not here. Not with everyone watching and listening. I grab the paint and raise the sleeve on his shirt. I know what the symbol is for his gift. I know it as well as I know my own.

"Vic give you a hard time?" he asks.

"That guy?" I say, pointing to Victor walking away. "Harmless."

Cody laughs in that way that means, *You don't know what you're talking about.*

"How are you?" I ask. I will my breath to calm down. I can hear the nerves in my voice making it shaky.

"Good," he says. "Why haven't you been answering my e-mails?"

He asks the question quietly, and I'm grateful, because all three of my friends are hanging around, eager to catch a snippet of anything he says to me.

"It's complicated." *I don't know what to say. I don't know if I can trust you with the truth about me.*

I take my time drawing his tattoo while we talk. It's good to talk to him again. It makes me wonder why I was keeping things from him.

I'm nearly done with Cody's tattoo when it happens.

Zena and Kendall show up.

They look like they just walked out of Buckle—blingy jeans with just the right wear in them (the kind you pay extra for), and even blingier shirts that put my outfit to shame.

Ivy rolls her eyes. "Prepare yourselves." The other girls at the booth giggle, and I smile at Ivy. It's good to know everyone else hates them too.

They spot our booth, but their eyes continue to scan the grounds. They have no intention of working tonight.

"They're looking for you," I tell him in a conspiratorial whisper.

"Hide me," he whispers back with a wink.

But I don't. I keep on painting and talking like normal.

As if drawn to him like a paper clip to a magnet, Kendall walks straight to Cody. She does a little throat-clearing thing to get Cody's attention, but he doesn't look. She finally steps in front of him, bumps me, and causes me to paint a line through Cody's symbol.

I step back, clean off the paintbrush, and ignore Kendall.

"You ready for some more dancing tonight?" her voice is too loud, her way of making sure everyone hears their conversation.

"I don't know," Cody answers. "Maybe."

He looks around her to find me, but she leans too, blocking me.

"You're a really good dancer," she says.

"Yeah, uh, thanks."

He stands up.

She looks surprised. I'm sure she expected him to flirt back; after all, that's what most guys do.

It's so funny, I almost laugh out loud.

"I've got to run, but—" He finally gets into a position where he can see me. "I'll be back in a bit to let you fix this."

Dru glares at Kendall. "How do you live with yourself?"

Kendall smoothes out the wrinkles in her shirt and ignores Dru's question. Dru just shakes her head.

Other guys walk up to the booth, each wanting their own tattoo. I have to shove Kendall out of the way to make room for the boy I'm going to paint. "If you aren't going to help, go away."

"Suits me," she says. She takes off with a deliberate toss of her hair that looks ridiculous. We all bust up laughing as she goes.

I spend the next two hours painting design after design. I keep looking for Cody but don't see him. There's an empty spot in my stomach that worries he's with Kendall or Zena.

A bell rings, and I know it's our signal to stop working the booths and gather for the ceremony. I put the lids on the paint containers and rinse the brushes so we can use them when this is over.

There are a lot of people here from other states. People just like us, it seems. I walk to the circle, looking for Ivy. She waves me over, and I walk in her direction. Someone grabs my arm as I walk by, and I spin to see who it is.

Cody.

"Where you going in such a hurry?" he asks. "Are you in the ceremony?"

I shake my head. "No, just looking for Ivy. I think I saw her over there." I point across the lawn.

"I'll come with you, if that's okay."

"Keep up," I tell him. I'm always nervous when I think about talking to Cody, but when I'm with him, that all goes away. Weird.

We find Ivy sitting with Dru and Jo and some guys Cody knows. The lights from the booths dim so that only candlelight illuminates the area beneath the giant oak tree's limbs. A series of chimes signals the beginning of the ceremony, and we face forward in our seats.

The headmistress climbs up the stairs to a small stage erected just for this purpose. She stands ten feet away, her dark hair smooth, her features impossibly perfect.

Her eyes survey the crowd in front of her. There must be close to a thousand people here. She looks more closely, sees me, then sees Cody. Her eyes, welcoming and kind just seconds ago, turn to cold, hard marbles.

She stares. And stares. And I know that if she could do so without making a scene, she would drag me inside by my new hair clip and tell me that I don't have time for a distraction like Cody.

But she can't say anything.

And she doesn't.

But it's coming.

She knows it. I know it. It's coming.

Twenty-Two

The ceremony takes longer than it should. By the time the headmistress begins to wrap up, everyone's antsy and I'm ready to get back to our booth. Based on the piercing glares from the headmistress throughout the ceremony, it's probably in my best interest to stay out of her way. She has no reason to be mad at me, unless she thinks my little rant to Kendall included her precious Zena. Or maybe she's just trying to intimidate me in the hopes I'll give up and let Kendall rule the coven. If her own daughter can't be High Priestess, then Kendall's the next best thing. I'm pretty sure the headmistress would eat toad guts before supporting me as High Priestess.

When the crowd breaks up, we decide to head back to our booth. Cody walks beside me, and the rest follow behind us. I feel self-conscious, like everyone is watching every single move we make.

"Well, that was interesting," Cody says. "A lot different than our ceremonies."

"Really? All of ours are pretty much the same. Almost identical, in fact. Change a chant here, add an element there, and voila! You have yourself a new ceremony. What are yours like?"

Cody's face is thoughtful. He finally settles on, "Darker." I'm about to ask him more questions, when he points to his arm. "Can you fix this?"

"Sorry about that," I tell him. "There's no stopping her when she's like that." That's what will make beating her for High Priestess such a challenge.

I lead him back to the booth and stop when it comes into view. Sitting on the chairs where our tattoo customers should be sitting are Kendall and Zena.

Cody laughs. "Should I come back later?"

I shake my head. "No," I say. I grab his hand and pull him toward the booth. I try to ignore the zing of nerves shooting straight from his hand to my heart. I shove the nerves down, determined to show Kendall she can't win this one.

Ivy walks up, puts her arm out to stop me. "I've got this," she says.

I walk slowly with Cody while Ivy and the girls walk ahead. Neither one of us breaks the hand-hold. I guess it's a good sign he didn't yank free the first chance he got.

Ivy stops at the chairs. "Get up."

Kendall and Zena keep talking, like Ivy isn't standing there.

Ivy puts her hands on her hips. I can practically hear her counting in her head.

"Get. Up."

Kendall finally looks at Ivy. "Make me."

"Oh no," I say under my breath. I half-walk, half-run to Ivy, and my hand slips from Cody's grasp. When I get to Ivy, Cody is right beside me.

"That's enough," I say to Kendall. I tip her chair forward so she has to get out.

Ivy says something to Zena under her breath. Whatever it is, it's scary enough to get Zena on her feet.

Cody doesn't make eye contact with either girl, and when they figure out he isn't going to, they stomp their way to the food booths. They laugh and talk about "the losers" (aka us) they're stuck with. There is so much I want to say to Kendall, but getting into a fight with her now will only embarrass me in front of Cody. I decide to take the high road, as Dad says, and act like she doesn't bother me. I look forward to the day when I truly don't care about Kendall.

I motion to Cody to sit down, and I reach for the paint remover.

"Those two are a handful," Cody remarks.

"That's one way of putting it," I tell him, smiling. I redo his tattoo, and it looks better than the first time I did it.

"You've got some real talent," Jo says.

I laugh. "Not hardly. Not like you, anyway."

Jo shoos me away with her hands. "Why don't you go get something to eat? You've been working the booth since we first got here."

"That sounds great," Cody says. "I'm starving. Want to go?"

I look at Jo, and her eyes are saying, *What are you waiting for?*

"I'll be back in a little bit," I promise.

"Take your time," Jo says. She looks at the row of empty seats. "It's not like we're busy."

Everyone must have eaten before the ceremony, because we're practically the only ones there. I get a salad, and Cody gets the biggest hot dog I've ever seen. He leads us to a table on the edge of the food area.

There's some awkward silence, and I have to fill it.

"Can we talk about the rumor?" I ask. "The one you said we had to talk about in person?"

Cody looks at me for a few long seconds. Then he looks around to see who can hear us. But there's no one near and no excuse to stall.

"It's hard to explain," he says.

"Try me."

He smiles at me. "Well, all right, then. I guess I will. What exactly did you hear again?"

I tell him about the rumor floating around Dowling, about him becoming High Priest when he turns twenty-one. While I tell him about the rumor, he nods, as if affirming each detail. With each nod my breathing ratchets up, my heart beats faster. When I'm done talking, he pops a chip into his mouth.

Then chews.

And chews.

And chews.

"Are you purposely dragging this out to test my patience?" I ask him.

He grins, still chewing. "Maybe," he says after swallowing.

I'm about to reach across the table and shake him. "So . . . care to answer me now?"

"You already know the answer," he says.

"If I knew the answer, I wouldn't be asking you."

"Trust your instincts, Hallie. What does your gut say?"

My initial reaction to the rumor was that it's bogus. But now . . . now that I know High Priests and Priestesses are determined by lineage and power, it seems more believable. I think about Cody and how he's behaved tonight. No one is telling him what to do; it's the other way around. But what does that really mean?

I look across the table at him and wrestle with my own secret. If he tells me, do I have to tell him? "I'm not sure if it's the same—"

Jo drops onto the bench beside me and slaps her hands onto the table. She's been running, and she's out of breath. "You're not going to believe this."

Dread's a heavy weight in my veins.

"What's wrong?" I ask. My voice is thin, and I hate

the way it sounds. If I'm going to fight to be the High
Priestess, I need to dig up some confidence.

When she opens her mouth, the words tumble out.
"I was washing the paintbrushes in the booth and heard
Kendall telling Zena that she has a plan to take care of you."

"What does that mean?" Cody asks. "What has to be
taken care of?"

Neither one of us answers.

"Did she say when?" I ask.

"Tonight."

"How?"

Jo looks at Cody.

"It's okay, Jo," I say. "You can say it in front of him."

She turns back to me. "She said they're going to burn
you out."

"Burn me out? What does that mean?"

I look to Cody, whose face has gone serious. I hardly
recognize his voice when he speaks. "Kendall said she
was going to do this? To Hallie? Tonight?"

"Yeah."

"Who else heard this?" Cody asks.

Jo shrugs. "Just me."

"And they didn't see you?" he asks.

I point to her ears. "Clairaudient."

Cody nods in understanding. "Thanks, Jo."

Realizing she's been dismissed, she walks back to the booth, looking over her shoulder at me several times. It's funny to watch Cody take charge. I have to get better at that. If I'm honest, it's kind of nice having someone around who seems to get what's happening. Because I'm lost.

"What's the story with those two? Why do they have it out for you?"

I hesitate. "I don't know."

Am I allowed to tell him about the High Priestess stuff? Or is it against the rules? I mean, he did tell me about his thing. Kind of.

"I can't help you if I don't know what's going on."

My first reaction is to tell him I don't need his help, but maybe I do. Maybe he knows what "burning" me out means. Surely one of my gifts can help me fight back.

I give Cody the short story of the quest for High Priestess. Cody nods while I talk, and I get the feeling he's memorizing every word I say.

When I finish, he takes a deep breath, then stands. "Come on."

I grab our trash and look for a Dumpster.

"Really, Hallie?" he asks. "We're in the middle of something kind of serious, and you're looking for a trash can?"

My face burns red, and I drop the trash onto the nearest table.

"Where would she be?" he asks.

"Who?" I ask.

Cody gives me an exasperated look. "Hallie, focus. Kendall. Where would she be right now?"

I look around the grounds, at the dwindling groups still here. Most of the out-of-town covens have already left.

"There," I say. I point at the stage, where Kendall and Zena are pretending to clean up.

He walks toward them with purpose, as if he can control them. Alone, they're formidable. Together, they're unbeatable.

"Wait. What's happening?" I ask. I grab his hand to stop his stride.

He stops walking but keeps his eyes on Kendall. "Burning you out means she's going to get rid of you."

"Like get me expelled? She'd never be able to. I'm their best student."

His eyes narrow, a mix of regret and anger. "No, Hallie. Something a lot more permanent than expulsion."

Twenty-Three

I swallow hard. I know Kendall doesn't like me, but would she really do something so drastic?

"How do you know so much?" I ask him.

"It's a long story."

I roll my eyes, more than a little tired of being put off by Cody. My eyes follow his to where the girls stand. They're watching the grounds, looks of superior satisfaction on their faces.

"I need to handle this on my own," I tell Cody.

He shakes his head. "No, you don't, Hallie. You can't. This is more than just mean-girl gossip."

"You think I don't know that?" I pull my hand out of his. "Let me do this."

I'll never be taken seriously if I can't fight my own battles.

Cody gets it, but he doesn't like it. "I'll be right here."

I walk to the stage, think about what to say. Should I be mean and threatening? Or just, "Hey! I heard you wanted to burn me out. Let's talk."

They watch me approach, the same satisfied grins on their faces, but I know there's malice behind their smiles.

"Hallie," Kendall says when I get close.

I study her face, looking for some sign of goodness in her.

I ask the one question I really want the answer to. "Why don't you like me?"

She tilts her head and looks at me like I'm a puzzle she can't quite figure out.

"Are you serious?" Her face is the picture of incredulity.

I have to stop myself from laughing. "Yeah, I really am. I've never done anything to you. But since third grade you've dedicated yourself to tearing me down."

A thin laugh escapes her lips. "Okaaaay, Hallie. I think you might be a little obsessed with me. I don't even *think* about you, much less 'tear' you down."

I look over to Cody, who's still watching us. He's no longer alone. One of his friends, Junior, and the first guy

I painted, Victor, are standing with him. Something like relief washes over me.

I take a deep breath, will my back to be ramrod straight. "And now you're mad at me about the High Priestess thing as if I applied for the job."

A slow, sinister smile creeps onto her face. "Ah, you're finally thinking."

"I don't understand why you're upset. It's not like I asked for this anyway. I just wanted to be a hedge witch."

"Poor Hallie," she sneers.

The chill in her words puts every nerve in my body on defense. My feet are telling me to run, but I know I have to face her about this. Might as well get it over with now.

Zena steps closer, her voice as menacing as I've ever heard.

"Understand this, Hallie. Dowling is too powerful a coven to be led by the likes of you—a Goody Two-shoes with overbearing parents and an unfortunate propensity for honesty."

"All things I'm proud of."

She laughs. "You would be." She leans closer, almost whispering into my ear. "Let me tell you what's going to happen here. You are going to step aside and let Kendall take her rightful place as the next High Priestess of the coven."

Anger boils inside me. "Why would I do that? I have as much right to that spot as Kendall."

"And then you're going to convince Cody that he belongs with Kendall."

I shake my head. I can't believe this. "He doesn't even like her."

"It really doesn't have anything to do with how he feels about her. This is about the continued partnership with Riley. Cody and Kendall are . . . destined to be together."

Destined to be together.

My dream comes back to me in flashes.

This is it.

This is what I was dreaming about.

"What genius decided those two belong together?" I ask her. My voice sounds a thousand times braver than I feel.

"The only one who matters." She points to herself. "My mom."

Pointless. This is entirely, hopelessly pointless. Nothing I say will change anything. If I'm going to be High Priestess, it will have to be in spite of the headmistress, her daughter, and Kendall.

I glance back at Cody, who's now surrounded by Ivy, Dru, and Jo. Even Missy is there. Kendall's eyes follow mine. "They can't help you."

"I don't need their help. I don't need anyone's help."

Miss A's colorful figure quickly approaches. I can tell by the look in her eyes that she aims to stop me from saying something I'll regret. She's probably too late for that.

I end the conversation by walking back to my friends. With every step, my legs shake harder and faster until I think I may actually fall down.

Then a flash of fire shoots past me and everything slips into slow motion.

Cody rushes toward me.

I turn around.

Another flash of fire. A fireball, to be exact.

Coming from Kendall's hand.

I should duck or run or scream. But instinct takes over, and I hold up my hands to shield my face.

In that weird way that happens only in near-death experiences, time practically stops. I see every revolution of the fireball. An inch from my hand it bounces off and shoots back toward Kendall.

With Miss A directly behind her.

Kendall ducks, yanking Zena down with her.

But Miss A is too slow, and the flame catches her flowing dress. She slaps frantic arms at the fire, but it doesn't extinguish. Ivy runs to Miss A, Missy trailing her.

Kendall holds up her hand, and I know another fireball is coming.

I see the fireball leave her hand, like a movie in super-slow motion.

I watch the fireball fly in Ivy's direction. But she isn't looking. I scream her name, she turns, and the fireball lands squarely in her stomach. She falls to the ground, smoke consuming her.

I look for my friends. Cody is running.

Running away.

That can't be right.

And then I see her.

Kendall.

Running to the front door. Zena trailing her.

And Cody is right behind them.

He grabs Kendall, and a man helps Cody by stopping Zena. I recognize him as the headmaster of Riley Academy.

I can't focus on them. I need to help Ivy.

My feet carry me faster than I thought possible. I

notice a crowd of girls circling Miss A, whose dress is flame-free thanks to Missy, who was able to turn it to ice, then melt it to douse the fire. Miss A is repeating the same thing over and over and over again. "I'm fine, girls. I'm fine."

I push people out of the way to reach Ivy, and find her unconscious. The fireball is gone, but smoke hangs overhead. I shake Ivy lightly, call her name. I tap her cheeks like I've seen people do on television, but she doesn't budge. She doesn't wake up.

Fear, despair, anger . . . it collides inside me, and I begin crying. I should have protected Ivy. I should have been more careful. How could I have underestimated Kendall?

"Miss A!" I yell for our dorm mother, Dowling's best hedge witch. If anyone can help my best friend, it's her.

Miss A stumbles through the crowd, mindless of the burned dress hanging off her in strips. She cares only about helping Ivy.

I push everyone back. Ivy would be mad if she knew everyone was just standing around looking at her. "Go on," I shout. "Go!"

Soon enough Jo and Dru have pushed everyone back

so that only Ivy, Miss A, Jo, Dru, Missy, and I are there. Miss A puts her hands on Ivy's stomach, begins chanting something low and soft and deep and healing.

She looks at me with a smile. "She's going to be all right, sugar. You need to calm down. She can feel your anxiety, remember?"

I nod, steady my breathing, and try to remember Miss A's power. I look in fear at my best friend lying on the ground in front of me, passed out and coughing.

Wait.

Coughing.

She's coughing!

"Ivy? Can you hear me?" I lean over her face and try to pull her eyes open with my fingers.

She slaps my hands away, and I nearly faint with relief.

I look to Miss A, who's still chanting, healing, smiling. She lifts Ivy's shirt, and all that remains of her fireball mishap is a red rash. "I told you she'd be okay."

Ivy's eyes open, slowly and carefully. She focuses on me, and I swear it looks like she's glaring at me.

"I don't blame you for being mad at me," I say. "I never should have confronted them like that. I wasn't thinking."

"I don't care about that," Ivy says.

I reach down and help her sit up. I don't think I've ever been so happy to see someone awake in my entire life.

"What I want to know," she says, "is why you didn't tell me you had the gift of shielding."

Twenty-Four

I stare at her, confused. The hit to the stomach must have twisted some things up in her head.

She coughs again, holds her stomach in pain.

"That's going to be sore awhile," Miss A says. She reaches for Ivy's hand and pulls her to her feet. "Why don't you sit down on those chairs for a few minutes, Ivy? Hallie, you stay with her. The girls and I have some work to do."

She motions for Jo, Dru, and Missy to follow her to the stage, where most of the damage from the fireball is.

I look for Cody but don't see him anywhere. Also missing are Kendall and Zena.

"So?" Ivy asks. "Why did you keep it a secret?"

"I have no idea what you're talking about."

"Really. You don't remember stopping the fireball with your bare hands?"

"I did?" I try to remember what happened. The fireball came toward me, and I lifted my hand. "I did! I held up my hand, and the fireball bounced off."

I don't say what I'm thinking, that I caused Miss A to catch fire, which caused Ivy to run to her and get hit by the fireball. It's times like these when I really wish I was just a regular witch. Or at least a white magic witch. Then my magic would actually help people, instead of hurting them.

Ivy pulls Lady Rose's barrette out of my hair. "Here," she says. "This was about to fall out."

I look at the barrette in my hand. At the red stones and the small clear crystals. It sparkles beneath the candlelight. When the realization hits me, I smile.

"This," I tell Ivy. "This is why I could shield myself from the fireball."

"A barrette?" she says, eyebrows drawn together. "What'd you do, steal it from the library?"

I don't answer right away, and she rips the barrette from my hand. "Are you kidding me? You actually took something again? You know what will happen. I can't believe you'd do this."

I slap a hand over her mouth. "Lady Rose gave it to me. She said it made her feel safer and that her grandmother had given it to her. Sneaky."

I guess this is what they kept warning me about. They knew something was going to happen but couldn't tell me, so they protected me the only way they could.

"You're lucky they like you. If they were like Kendall, you'd be toast right now."

"Literally," I say. We both laugh, and even when Ivy holds her stomach in pain, we keep laughing.

I put Ivy to bed and head back outside to clean up. I'm disappointed I didn't get to tell Cody good-bye. I owe him a huge thank-you for chasing after Kendall and Zena. I don't know where they were running to, but he stopped them, and I'm grateful.

Only a few dozen girls are still on the grounds. Some are stacking chairs, some removing candles, some picking up trash. I stand at the top of the stairs and watch them work together, and I feel isolated, separate from everyone else.

I wonder if I'll make it through Dowling. I used to just "know" I'd be fine, but now I'm not so sure. Do I even *want* to continue here? Nothing I do works out the way I plan. The people closest to me get hurt.

"Now you're just being silly." Miss A puts an arm around my shoulders.

For once I'm glad she heard my thoughts. I wouldn't have had the guts to say them out loud.

"I don't know, Miss A. Think about it. Nothing I attempt to do works out like it should. It was one thing when Kendall got a forked tongue. But now you and Ivy got hurt. I don't want that to happen ever again."

She puts her hands on my shoulders and turns me around to face her. Her makeup has melted off her face, and what's beneath is a determined and intelligent woman. I wonder why she puts on so much makeup and dresses so outrageously. She's better like this. When she's just . . . her. Miss A.

"Now, you listen to me, little girl. What happened tonight was not your fault. No, ma'am. That was Kendall's and Zena's fault, and if I had my way, I'd make sure they never stepped foot in Dowling again."

"Where are they?" I ask. "I haven't seen them since . . ." I don't finish the sentence. I can't.

"Since Ivy was hit?" she asks. "You can talk about it. It's okay."

I nod, unconvinced, and repeat my question. "Where are Kendall and Zena?"

"In their room," Miss A says with a shake of her head.

"What's going to happen now?" I ask her. "Will I get . . . expelled? Suspended?"

The thought of calling my dad and telling him I was kicked out of Dowling gives me a headache. He would be devastated. As would I. If I don't stay—if I *can't* stay—I think I'll always wonder what my life would have been like. And I think that would be an awful way to live.

Miss A chuckles, and it makes me grin. "Expelled? Not hardly. It was self-defense, my dear." She gives me a wink. I smile even though I know I shouldn't.

"You know, Hallie, you don't have to go through this alone."

"Through what?"

"The High Priestess competition. You don't have to do it alone. I will help you. Lady Jennica and Lady Rose will too. I don't think you should expect any help from the headmistress, though." She laughs at her joke, and I laugh with her.

"Do you really think I could do it? That I could be the High Priestess?" Just saying it out loud sounds absurd, like I'm asking if I could be a two-headed purple-and-green giraffe that survived on lollipops and cotton candy.

"Well, of course I do, darlin'. So does everyone else."

Except a few, I think.

"Those few don't matter," she tells me. "But I'll tell you one thing. You have absolutely got to figure out how to lock up those thoughts so other people can't hear them. That could be dangerous with the wrong person."

The scratch of shoes on concrete interrupts us.

I turn around and see Cody on the step below me.

My heart shoots past normal and jumps into high gear.

"Well, that garbage isn't going to pick itself up, now is it?" Miss A walks away, her burned muumuu having been replaced by oversize sweat pants and a large T-shirt with butterflies painted all over it. She waves her hand above her head. "Bye, Cody!"

"Bye, Miss A," he calls, laughing. "She's something else."

I smile and nod. "She's perfect."

"Speaking of perfect," he says.

I'm so tired, I can't think clearly. "Perfect?"

"Yeah," he says. "That'd be you."

I stare at him for several seconds, and then explode with laughter. "Me?" I ask through tears. "Perfect? You can't . . . be . . . serious."

He puts his hands into his pockets and smiles at me. "Very funny."

"Well, come on," I tell him. "That was hilarious. Did you see what I did tonight?"

"What you did?"

"How I almost burned Miss A to a crisp? And nearly killed my best friend by drilling a fiery hole through her?"

He shakes his head like he's trying to clear cobwebs. "What I saw was a girl defending herself, then rescuing her best friend."

"That's just the thing, Cody. The fireballs wouldn't have even happened if I hadn't started the argument with Kendall."

"Maybe not today, but it would have happened another day. Don't deny it. You know I'm right."

I think about what he's said. He might be right. I don't think I could have gone much longer without confronting her. "Still . . . it was reckless to do it here, at the celebration, where other people could get hurt."

"I'm glad it happened tonight. I got to see what you

can do, and let me tell you, Hallie. You've got some mad skills."

Embarrassment warms my face, my chest. Thank goodness it's dark out.

"You were like Wonder Woman out there."

I laugh. "Yeah. Stopping a fireball. That was a new one for me tonight. Came in handy, though." I make a mental note to do something special for the two teachers who helped me.

We stand in the quiet, watching the others clean up. It's surreal to think about what happened tonight. It seems more like a movie than reality. *Life is stranger than fiction,* I hear my dad say.

That's when I notice that all the buses are gone. "Where's your bus?" I ask.

"The headmaster let me stay behind with him. He had to do something with the headmistress. Make some report or something."

"Witches make reports?" I ask. For some reason that strikes me as really funny, and I laugh.

Cody laughs with me, and we both relax. "Sorry we didn't get to spend more time together," he says.

"At least I kept you entertained."

"There's that," he agrees. "You're cool, Hallie. I like hanging out with you."

My tongue is literally stuck to the roof of my mouth, like I just ate a glob of peanut butter. Or superglue.

Say something. Anything!

"Me too." I hear the words come out of my mouth, and immediately I want to rewind time and have a do-over. *Me too?* Brilliant, Hallie. You're a regular Shakespeare.

Silence. Not uncomfortable. But silence. And I have to fill it.

"When's our next thing together?" I ask.

Cody shrugs. "Not sure. December, I think."

December.

As in two months away.

"E-mail until then?" he asks.

I look at Cody's face, so perfect, so honest. I *really* like him. But I'm too chicken to say it out loud. Why would he choose to like me? I'm a black magic witch with powers I can't control, headed for a future I'm not sure I can handle or even want.

But here he is. Smiling at me. I don't know why, but he likes me too.

"E-mail until then," I say.

Before I even know what I'm doing, I lean forward and give him such a quick kiss, I'm not even sure our lips actually touch.

I don't wait for him to say something, just walk down the stairs to the lawn. I'm halfway down the steps when Cody calls my name.

I turn around, smile. "Yeah?"

"It's true," he says. "The rumor? It's true."

I give him a thumbs-up, then go to help Miss A.

I can feel his eyes follow me as I walk away, something that would normally make me nervous. But now . . . now it's just right. Like this is the beginning of something wicked good.

Don't miss how it all began!
Read on for a peek at
The XYZs of Being Wicked.

One

Mom's voice is clipped and irritated when she taps her watch. "Tick tock, Hallie."

I keep my eyes on the television. "When this is over."

The television clicks off, and I huff out a big breath. I hate it when she does that.

"I'm not packing for you, no matter how long you put it off."

I lie down on the couch and groan. "I'll do it later. Who knows when I'll get to see my shows again."

"One, two . . ."

"Really? You're counting? I'm eleven, Mom. Not five."

She grabs my legs and drops them to the floor. "Now."

Moving more slowly than honey in a snowstorm, I drag myself to the attic door.

I hate attics. And basements. They're the soulless pits of a house, and I have no use for either one of them. Except today. Today, I *have* to climb into the attic. It doesn't matter that the last time I was in the attic, I fell and landed face-first in the biggest spiderweb any spider has ever created in the history of the world.

I'm on my third jump to reach the cord hanging from the attic door when Dad appears. He drops a step ladder in front of me. "The definition of 'insanity' is doing the same thing and—"

"Expecting different results," I finish. Dad's a total quote junkie. This particular Einstein quote has been repeated in my house so many times, I have it memorized.

I take two steps on the small ladder, grab the cord, and pull it down.

"Packing? Already?" he teases, knowing Mom's been nagging me for a week to pack.

"Funny, Dad." I give him a smile, and my heart pinches. I'm going to miss him. I'm going to miss Mom. I'm going to miss my dog, Charlie. The only thing I won't miss is the heartless Kendall Scott, who has made it her personal mission in life to ensure I never rise above the level of social scum at school.

Dad rubs his hands together like he's warming them over a fire. "Exciting stuff, Hallie."

A flame of panic spreads through my stomach. I douse it with the reminder that I'm starting over in a new school with new kids. Dowling's my do-over.

I look up the attic stairs, then back at him. He knows how I feel about attics. "Want me to turn the light on?" Without waiting for me to answer, he climbs the stairs, yanks the light cord, and comes back down. "It's all yours."

Watching Dad walk off, I wish I'd asked him to go up with me. I grab the handle of the folding stairs that lead to the attic and gently place my foot on the first step. It creaks lightly under my weight.

You're being ridiculous, Hallie Faith Simon. Climb the steps, clean out the trunk, pack, and be done with it.

I hold my breath and take the rest of the steps quickly, exhaling when I reach the top. The attic is as musty and menacing as I remember.

I scan the neatly stacked boxes, plastic tubs, and plywood walking paths. I place one foot on the wood to test its strength, then gingerly walk the plank. The trunk is exactly where Mom said it would be—under the window, covered in dust, daring me to open it.

I drop to my knees and blow on the top of the trunk. Even after I open the window, the dust hangs in the air and I have to wave my hands in front of me to see better. Putting my hand on the metal latch, I close my eyes, and quickly lift the lid. When nothing jumps out and kills me, I peek through one eye to examine the trunk. Seems safe enough, so I dare to open both eyes. Carved on the inside of the lid is something I can't read. I trace my fingers over the cursive letters and try to pronounce the words.

Delicias fuge ne frangaris crimine, verum
Coelica tu quaeras, ne male dipereas;
Respicias tua, non cujusvis quaerito gesta
Carpere, sed laudes, nec preme veridicos;
Judicio fore te praesentem conspice toto.

Anxiety swims through me. I may not be able to read it, but I know these words will be important in my new world. Engraved below that are words I can actually read.

SIMON FAMILY TRUNK
DOWLING ACADEMY SCHOOL OF
WITCHCRAFT, Est. 1521

More curious than afraid, I peer into the trunk. Part of me hopes there's a copy of *Witchcraft for Dummies* inside, but all I find are two weird things that look like they belong in a museum.

A small stick that looks like a miniature totem pole leans in the corner of the trunk. Again I blow the dust off and lean in for a closer look. But I can't see it the way I want and slowly slip my hand into the trunk. I grab the stick and pull it out quickly, like rattlers are threatening to strike. When lightning doesn't fry me, I let out the breath I've been holding. Call me crazy, but digging in a dead witch's trunk puts this girl on edge.

The stick is so light, I can barely feel it in my hands as I hold it up to the sunlight. Symbols I don't recognize are carved into the stick, and instead of totally creeping me out, it calms me. I can't explain it, but something like relief washes over me.

I put the stick back into the trunk, and, braver than I thought possible, I grab the only other item in the trunk. A book of yellowed pages with an *S* embossed in the center fills my hands. I wipe the black leather cover and let my finger trace the *S*. Is the *S* for "Simon"?

Gently I open the cover and read the inscription.

This Book of Shadows Belongs to Elsa Whittier Simon.

I grin at the small angry letters scribbled at the bottom.

HANDS OFF!

I don't make friends easily, but I think I would have liked my great-great-grandmother.

I reread the inscription. *Book of Shadows.* Another part of my new life I know nothing about. Thumbing through the pages filled with perfect cursive handwriting, I stop at a dog-eared page.

> Hear us now, the words of the witches,
> The secrets we hide in the night.
> Our magic is sought,
> Invoke our power,
> In this hour,
> On this night.

I whisper the words as I read them, over and over again.
"Hal?"
The sound of my mother's voice behind me stops my

heart for a full second. I whip my head around, but before I can tell her how badly she scared me, wind swirls inside the attic, first soft and refreshing. Then churning faster and faster and faster, like an angry tornado. Boxes, papers, and pieces of insulation hurl through the room so fiercely, I can barely hold my place on the floor. I clutch the Book of Shadows to my chest to keep from losing it.

I attempt to scream through the storm. "Mom!"

The trunk seems to be the only thing not flying through the room, so I grab it in a death grip.

There's no reply from Mom, and I've lost sight of her in the storm debris.

My glasses begin sliding from my face, and I drop the Book of Shadows to hold them in place.

In that instant the room stills.

My eyes dart through the room, taking in the attic, the attic that should be filled with trash but looks exactly as it did when I first climbed the stairs.

Hand still clamped on the trunk, I take a shaky breath. What in the world just happened? Did I imagine it?

When I finally lock eyes with Mom, her body is frozen in fear.

No. I did not imagine this. What just happened scared

her even more than it terrified me, and I remind myself that she's as new to this as I am.

"What— Did you— How . . ." She stutters over her words, trying to make sense of the bizarro scene. All the relief I felt just moments ago has evaporated, and in its place is sheer panic.

I can't do this.

I can't do this.

I can't be a witch.

But a voice thunders in my head. *I have to do this.*

I toss the book into the trunk and shut the lid before dragging the piece of luggage closer to Mom. I need to get out of here and immediately pretend none of it happened, pretend I didn't cause the storm, and pretend I'm not going to a school for witches.

"See?" I say. "Didn't I tell you? Nothing good happens in attics."

Two

Standing in the registration line at Dowling, I struggle to keep a sweaty grip on my side of the family trunk. Dad's holding the other side, shoulders back, chest out, pride spewing out of him like an erupting volcano.

I grow more anxious as each minute passes. I was flabbergasted when my parents told me about Dowling and why I had to go. How could I have been a witch my whole life and never known? Dad's explanation involving lineage and some great-great-grandmother I never met made little sense. But I knew he was telling the truth. And I knew I had to go, no matter how badly I wanted to stay in my safe, predictable world.

There's only one girl in front of us. Like me, she's

in jeans, a red polo, and white shoes. Like me, she's white-knuckling one end of her family trunk, pretending there's nowhere else she'd rather be.

Finished signing in, the family follows an older Dowling student down a wide hallway. I steel myself for the reality that my parents are about to walk me to my dorm. Then leave. For good.

I trudge up to the table and come face-to-face with a plump woman with a bright smile and curly hair so dry, it looks like it could catch fire at any moment. I make a mental note of the name on her ID badge. Agnes Armstrong.

I take her in. Mascara is caked in globs on her short, stumpy eyelashes, and the deep red lipstick smeared across her lips has smudged onto her teeth. It's kind of a mess but somehow seems right on her.

"Well, hello there!" she says. "What's your name, sugar?"

I pull my eyes from her red-stained choppers. "Hallie. Hallie Simon."

Her eyes brighten and she raises her hand in the air. I just stare at it, confused. Surely she isn't trying to high-five me.

"You're one of my girls!" she announces, bouncing in her seat.

Since I have no idea what it means to be one of her girls, I just smile.

She waves her hand closer to me. "Well, don't leave me hanging."

I tap my hand to hers, quick as I can. In my old school, public high-fiving is a one-way ticket to merciless mocking.

"What does it mean, exactly, when you say Hallie is one of your girls?" Mom puts her hand on my shoulder, pulling me closer.

Miss Armstrong slaps her hands to her chest. "Where are my manners! I just get so excited when I meet my girls for the first time." She focuses her attention on me. "I'm your dorm mother, sweetie. I'll be your mom away from home."

Mom's hand tightens on my shoulder.

"If you're sick," she says, "I'll be the one to give you that TLC. Although . . ." Her brows draw together like she's realizing something for the first time. "I can't recall the last time a student fell ill at Dowling. Hmm. Curious."

"Excellent to hear." Dad shoots his hand in front of him. I brace myself for his booming salesman voice. "Phil Simon."

I cringe, waiting for Miss Armstrong's reaction.

"Well, now, isn't that a nice howdy-do!" she says, pumping his hand firmly. "Agnes Armstrong," she answers, the tone of her voice mimicking Dad's. She shifts her focus back to me. "But you can call me Miss A. All the girls do."

Miss A passes Mom a business card. "Now, I don't want you to worry about a thing. You can reach me anytime, night or day. Just call that number, and whatever you do, don't forget the code. I can't talk to you unless you have the code, even if I recognize your voice." She shakes her head abruptly. "No exceptions."

"What's the code?" Panic makes Mom's voice a little louder, a little more forceful, than usual.

"It's printed in the bottom right-hand corner. See it?"

I lean closer and see the small series of letters and numbers that seem to squirm and shift on the paper. The harder I look at the numbers, the more they seem to morph, to change. An 8 turns into an *S* and a *T* turns into a 7.

"Yeah, I see it." Mom looks at me, her face a jumbled mess of worry, confusion, and run-for-your-life fear.

"Now, let's see here," Miss A says, dragging a stubby finger down a sheet of blank paper in front of her. I shift so I can get a better look at the paper, but no matter which direction I move, the paper remains blank. If it *is* blank, what in the world is she looking at?

"Nope! Your roommate hasn't arrived yet. But I'm sure she'll be here lickety-split."

She grabs a large white envelope from a box beside her chair. She slides her hand across the envelope, and my name appears in perfect, fancy handwriting.

Or was it already there? Maybe I need new glasses.

"Here you go, Hallie. You don't want to lose this, so take special care that you don't misplace it when you unpack. It includes your daily schedule and, most important, the dining hall schedule. Be sure you make it for meals. After hours the kitchen is locked up tighter than Alcatraz."

"There will be plenty of choices for her, correct?" Mom asks.

"She's vegetarian," Dad adds, lowering his voice to a whisper. He hates that I'm vegetarian. He doesn't understand how anyone can survive without meat. Maybe it's my hedge witch ancestry, but I have a thing for organically grown vegetables. It's one of the many things Kendall used to tease me about.

Miss A gives a double thumbs-up. "Yes, ma'am!"

She hands me a beaded lanyard that reminds me of

the necklace I got when we visited an Indian reservation in Louisiana. No two stones are the same, and they have a tribal look to them.

Hanging from the lanyard is an ID card. Dead center is a picture of me I've never seen, wearing the exact same shirt I'm wearing now. I mentally backtrack through the last few months. Did I try this shirt on before today? Did Mom take my picture? I know that I know that I *know* . . . I didn't put this shirt on before today. So that means they took this picture . . . today? How? When? And how'd it get on my badge so quickly?

Aladdin M!X
Collect them all!

DOWNLOAD A COMPLETE M!X CHECKLIST AT ALADDINMIX.COM.

EBOOK EDITIONS ALSO AVAILABLE

m!x | FROM ALADDIN | KIDS.SIMONANDSCHUSTER.COM